The Black Ace moved toward Bolan. "They call me Stone. And you are?"

"Omega," Bolan replied.

The gray-eyed gunner frowned as he tried to recall the name. "Can't say I've heard of you, but what the hell. I guess you won't mind if I check your card."

Bolan had a heartbeat to decide if he should bolt or play out the hardman's game.

Stone took the plastic ace of spades and scrutinized it closely. Then he looked up and glared at Scarpato. "You look at this?"

The New York mobster shook his head. "They cleared him at the gate."

Stone handed the calling card to Vince Scarpato, then turned to face the Executioner.

"It's bogus, Vince. You've got a ringer on your hands...."

D0324739

MACK BOLAN

The Executioner

DON PENDLETON's EXECUTIONER

MACK BOLAN

Missouri Deathwatch

A GOLD EAGLE BOOK FROM

W🌐RLDWIDE

TORONTO · NEW YORK · LONDON · PARIS
AMSTERDAM · STOCKHOLM · HAMBURG
ATHENS · MILAN · TOKYO · SYDNEY

First edition November 1985

ISBN 0-373-61083-1

Special thanks and acknowledgment to
Mike Newton for his contributions to this work.

Copyright © 1985 by Worldwide Library.
Philippine copyright 1985. Australian copyright 1985.

All rights reserved. Except for use in any interview, the
reproduction or utilization of this work in whole or in part
in any form by any electronic, mechanical or other means,
now known or hereafter invented, including xerography,
photocopying and recording, or in any information storage
or retrieval system, is forbidden without the permission
of the publisher, Worldwide Library, 225 Duncan Mill Road,
Don Mills, Ontario, Canada M3B 3K9.

All the characters in this book have no existence outside the
imagination of the author and have no relation whatsoever to
anyone bearing the same name or names. They are not even
distantly inspired by any individual known or unknown to the
author, and all the incidents are pure invention.

The Worldwide Library trademarks consisting of the words
GOLD EAGLE and THE EXECUTIONER are registered
in the United States Patent Office and in the Canada Trade
Marks Office. The Gold Eagle design trademark, the Executioner
design trademark, the Mack Bolan design trademark, the globe
design trademark, and the Worldwide design trademark
consisting of the word WORLDWIDE in which the
letter "O" is represented by a depiction of a globe are
trademarks of Worldwide Library.

Printed in Canada

To the families of the 2,489 MIAs who keep the candle in the window. Keep the flame burning bright!

Cowards die many times before their deaths;
The valiant never taste of death but once.
Of all the wonders that I yet have heard,
It seems to me most strange that men should fear;
Seeing that death, a necessary end,
Will come when it will come.

—Shakespeare: *Julius Caesar*, ii, 2, 1599

My death, when it comes, will not be premature.
And I'll be going out fighting.

—Mack Bolan

PROLOGUE

Mack Bolan stood atop a bluff, gazing at the broad Mississippi. At his back the midnight lights of St. Louis silhouetted him against the velvet sky. And on his hilltop perch the man in black could feel a stirring of the city's ghosts.

The Executioner knew this town, this battlefield, from personal experience. A bitter skirmish in his private war against the Mafia had been enacted here—how many lives ago?

It seemed a thousand years...and only yesterday.

Chuck Newman's urgent message had been channeled to the warrior through his brother, Johnny, and it was enough to bring Bolan back to these killing fields where so much blood had been spilled out in the pursuit of his long crusade. To see, perhaps, if the St. Louis soil was thirsty once again.

Chuck Newman had been an up-and-coming politician, favored as a candidate for governor, when members of the Mafia discovered certain indiscretions by his wife. A would-be actress in her younger days, she had appeared in certain films that would have, if aired in public, scuttled any hopes her husband cherished for elective office. Newman had got in touch with Able Team—a slick investigative outfit in those days before the terrorist wars—and thus Mack Bolan was attracted to St. Louis, carrying the cleansing fire.

Between them, Bolan, Schwarz and Blancanales had broken the chains that held Chuck Newman. He had retired from politics and concentrated on the law, advancing in a few short years to reach the upper strata of Missouri law enforcement.

Building on the lessons learned from Bolan, he had dealt some telling blows against the hoodlums of the Show Me State, recording some convictions that had drawn attention from the media...and won him mention as a candidate for transfer to the Justice camp, in Washington.

But there was trouble again in St. Louis, and when Newman found himself beyond his depth, he sent a message out along familiar channels. Word reached Able Team, already occupied with other tasks, and it had been relayed to Johnny Bolan, at the San Diego Strongbase. The younger Bolan listened, understood and made the call.

Dusty phantoms were stirring to life, their chains already clanking in the soldier's mind. No victory could ever stay absolutely won in everlasting war. Frustration was a constant in Mack Bolan's private war. He learned to live with it, to make the most of what he had when time and circumstance allowed.

But victory—that exhilarating moment when the last foe sprawls before you in the dust and no more rise to take his place—was ever and eternally beyond his reach. The Executioner was doomed to fight a grim containing action—striking lethal blows against the savages wherever they appeared, but never damming the tide of new replacements who replenished the hostile ranks.

His enemy was Savage Man, and the battlefield was everywhere. Bolan was historian enough to know that his crusade was not a new idea.

The struggle had been going on since prehistoric times, and it would not be finally decided by the outcome of a skirmish on the Mississippi.

But he had to try.

It was his destiny.

And it was time to do it all again in old St. Louis. This time maybe it would stick.

Mack Bolan turned his back on the silent river, put the overlook behind him, moving out to join the ghosts.

He owed it to them.

And to himself.

Okay, more from the beginning, with feeling.

From the heart.

1

The guard dog never knew what hit him. For an instant, he was on alert, every sense attuned to something strange on his turf. At first, it was no more than a smell, fleeting, but lingering in his cerebral cortex long enough to set alarm bells jangling and raise the bristle hairs along his spine. The night eyes could detect a shadow movement now, and he was snarling, circling to face the intruder, when there was a gentle popping sound and a sudden stinging pain against his flank.

The dog sat down, his hind legs suddenly refusing to obey the fevered brain's command. He felt the darkness closing in, and he was whimpering now, afraid, incapable of understanding as it carried him away.

The shepherd was inert and breathing softly by the time Mack Bolan reached him, already tucking the Crossman Pellgun away in his web belt. He used a moment to retrieve the tranquilizer dart and run a hand along the guard dog's muscled flank in mute apology.

The dog had been responding to his instincts and the training that had turned him from a gentle family pet to something swift and sinister. This animal was not the enemy, but they were close now. Bolan felt their nearness as he merged with darkness, homing on his primary objective.

The Executioner was dressed to kill, his blacksuit clinging to him like a second skin, the hidden pockets filled with slim stilettos, wire garrotes and other tools of silent death. The sleek Beretta 93-R nestled in its armpit sheath, and the silver AutoMag, Big Thunder, rode its thunder spot on Bolan's hip in military leather. Canvas pouches circling his waist held extra magazines for both weapons, interspersed with hand grenades arranged to let him pick them out by touch alone.

The soldier came prepared for a soft probe this time out. Still he knew from grim experience how chance and circumstance could foil the best-laid plans of any warrior, turning a soft probe into something hard and deadly. He was navigating by ear this time, and he was primed to kill if he encountered any solid opposition on the way.

The grounds were familiar to him from another visit, in another lifetime. Closing on his target, Bolan reached the wall, melding with the midnight shadows to scrutinize the house some fifty yards away.

The crumbling estate was situated in a small, exclusive neighborhood on the city's west side, nestled among the mansions of the nouveaux riches. It struck Bolan that the aging palace was symbolic of the empire it had come to represent. Already weakened—superficially, at least—by weather and the ravages of time, it seemed an easy mark.

But the warrior knew a dragon dwelled within those walls, and age had not entirely robbed it of its fire. The Executioner was well aware that overconfidence had killed more soldiers in the field than any other single enemy, and he was not about to join their ranks.

Bolan had a good view of the house—its broad front doors, one side, a portion of the glassed-in porch out back. Beyond his line of sight would be the swimming pool and sauna, tennis courts—unused for years—and private putting green. The carport, with its pair of carbon-copy Continentals, was positioned to the rear at the end of a looping, graveled driveway.

On his first invasion of the dragon's lair so long ago, Bolan had entered by the porch, but now he focused full attention on an upstairs window, which showed muted light through the draperies. Giamba's study would be there, unless the aging don had gone in for remodeling of late…and Bolan's instincts told him nothing much had changed inside the manor house.

He eyed the trellis that rose to a balcony above, and knew that he could scale it if it would bear his weight. The problem would be getting there, with fifty yards of open ground between him and the house, a free-fire zone where he would be exposed to any errant sentry, any watcher from a darkened window, scanning for intruders on the grounds.

He had encountered no resistance yet except the dog, and Bolan wondered if Giamba's own survival sense was failing in his twilight years. There might be hidden guards, of course, and yet he had to take a chance.

The warrior had not come this far to let the opportunity escape. He needed to obtain a handle on the situation in St. Louis, and Giamba could provide the necessary insight.

A final scan to either side, and Bolan made his break, a darting shadow that erupted from the base of the wall. He crossed the lawn with loping strides, quickly merging with the darkness pooled around the manor house itself. Here, huddled in a combat crouch, while respiration normalized, the numbers running down without a cry of warning in the night.

When he was satisfied, the soldier made another sprint toward the trellis, pausing once again for safety's sake before he reached up and tugged at the wooden structure, testing it with his weight. It held and Bolan scrambled upward with the practiced movements of an acrobat. He scaled the railing of the balcony, and flattened up against the wall beside the sliding windows.

Another breathless moment, waiting to discern if hearing more acute than Art Giamba's had detected his arrival. There was no sound beyond the glass. He tried the sliding window, found it locked and knew that he would have to force his way inside the study.

A slim stiletto filled his hand, and he was bending toward the window latch when headlights flashed along the curving drive. Bolan sought the shadows and watched as two sleek limousines pulled up outside Giamba's door, their lights and engines killed in unison.

He moved to peer across the rail, already counting as the Cadillacs began disgorging men and guns. He tallied six, added the wheelmen, and came up with a hit team.

Whatever had been going on around St. Louis before, the heart of it was coming down right here, right now. And Art Giamba was about to entertain, some unexpected callers.

As he wondered how this crew had gotten through the gate, he heard a door opening below him. A startled voice was barking questions, and then the muffled chug of silenced automatic pistols answered the houseman's challenge.

Four of the intruders disappeared inside, their backups seeming almost relaxed as they leaned against the cars, their weapons dangling at their sides. They were professionals and everything about them told him they had come expecting nothing in the way of true resistance.

Muffled shouting now, a single shot within the house, and then the four emerged carrying a fifth man. Despite the semidarkness and the altitude, the rumpled hair and smear of blood that masked his profile, Bolan recognized the mafioso he had come to see.

And Art Giamba was in trouble.

Again.

A sense of déjà vu was nagging at the Executioner, but he had no time to sit back and think it through. He had to act, or watch his "handle" disappear before he had a chance to gather the intelligence he needed for his own campaign.

They reached the cars, and Artie was propelled into the back seat of the Caddy first in line. The Executioner was out of numbers, and he would have to make his move right now or let it go.

He moved, vaulting the railing of the balcony, a grenade with pin released now in his hand. With half a heartbeat left to touchdown, Bolan pitched the fragger. He registered explosive impact on the second Caddy's windshield, startled hands upraised to shield the driver's face from flying glass, and then the warrior's mind was fully occupied with grim survival.

Bolan landed squarely on the point car's roof and used it as a springboard, dropping out of sight behind the tank before the startled gunners had a chance to realize what was happening. He hit a combat crouch, the sleek Beretta in his hand, and he was ready when smoky thunder tore the night apart.

The second crew wagon exploded, raining shattered safety glass on the estate grounds. The thunderclap swallowed up the driver's dying screams as flames licked at empty window frames, the front doors flapping from the shock waves like a dying condor's wings.

The first concussion flattened three of Bolan's opposition, and the rest were scrambling away from the heat and shrapnel, when the soldier showed himself, Beretta braced in both hands, tracking into target acquisition. The leader of the team was swiveling to meet a different kind of heat. The silenced autoloader chugged its greetings, opening up a vent between the startled eyes. The gunner toppled backward, lifeless, and Bolan pivoted to bring another target under fire.

The second mark was lining up an Army-issue .45, already squeezing off when Bolan's parabellum mangler drilled his jaw, boring on to clip his spine and lodge between the lumbar vertebrae. The .45 roared and Bolan felt the bullet's passage only inches from his face as he moved into confrontation with another target.

The standing gunner held a stubby shotgun in his hands, the cut-down muzzle leveled square at Bolan. And at this range he wouldn't have to aim to take out his target, providing that he got the chance.

A fleeting movement in the corner of his eye distracted Bolan for a moment, and he registered the Caddy's driver struggling to free himself from the entanglements of seat belt, steering wheel, the Colt revolver in his fist forgotten briefly as he wrestled with his door. Another instant, and he was free, lurching from his seat and circling around the open door to face the warrior, precisely as the shotgun man behind him opened fire.

The buckshot scarcely had a chance to spread before it struck the wheelman, crucifying him against the Caddy's fender. The life had flickered out behind his bulging eyes before he fell away, and Bolan was already sighting down the black Beretta's slide, when a secondary detonation from the dying tail car's gas tank rocked him, spewing liquid fire in streamers through the night.

The standing gunner became a dancing human torch, the stubby scattergun discarded as he stumbled back and forth, attempting to beat out the fire with blistered hands. His wailing voice was like an echo out of hell.

A gentle squeeze, and the Beretta bucked in Bolan's fist. A parabellum round punched in between the ovaled lips, imparting mercy to a tortured soul. The blazing scarecrow melted backward, throwing off a shower of sparks as he touched down on the driveway.

Bolan circled the tank, slid behind the wheel and cranked the big V-8 to life. He had not planned to exit from Giamba's hardsite in a set of stolen wheels, much less with any passenger in tow, but circumstances had been altered radically by the arrival of the hit team. From here on out, until they found a temporary haven from the hostile guns, the soldier would be running on his instincts.

Fighting for his life.

Bolan dropped the Caddy into gear and powered out of there, the tail car's funeral pyre a dwindling beacon in his rearview mirror as he held the pedal down along the drive. He left the lights off, navigating by the moonlight filtering through the overhanging trees.

A short two hundred yards until they reached the gates, and he would see then whether they were clear or if they had a fight in store for them. If the gorillas at the house had backups on the gate, there might be no escape.

He shrugged, and concentrated on his driving, on the figure slumped across the back seat, showing signs of life.

It would be Bolan's task to keep that life secure, at least until he had the answers he required.

If he could get them off the ground and find a temporary shelter for the mafioso.

If he did not lose his own life in the process.

It was a challenge, and the Executioner would meet it in the only way he knew.

Head-on.

2

With fifty yards to freedom, he kicked the headlights on to high beam, illuminating gate and guardhouse, trees and undergrowth, a stretch of manicured lawn. If there was any ambush there, the soldier wanted time enough to take evasive action before the gunners opened fire.

Nothing.

Wrought-iron gates were standing unattended, open on the night. Alert to any sign of treachery, he slowed his charger long enough to take a look around.

And on his first scan Bolan spied the gateman lying off to one side, his body tucked away beneath a hedgerow. Blood was seeping through the khaki uniform where half a dozen slugs had punctured flesh and fabric.

The hit team would have taken him before he had a chance to warn the house of their approach. It would explain their entry to the grounds, and the advantage of surprise that had defeated Art Giamba's housemen.

It explained a lot of things, except why they wanted Artie, or who they were....

Had been, he corrected himself. The hungry guns weren't anybody now.

Bolan and his passenger swept past the gateman's body, accelerating as the Caddy's tires encountered pavement, gaining traction now that they were finally off the gravel driveway. Turning left toward town, he stood on the accelerator, laying rubber as he put Giamba's house of death behind him.

But they did not make their exit unobserved.

Ahead, a pair of headlights flared, and Bolan recognized the backup limousine at once, its sleek shape sinister beneath the street lamps. It was only common sense for them to stake out the grounds, watch for any late arrivals, stragglers escaping from the strike.

The headlights flashed once, again...a prearranged signal, sure. The soldier wasted no time trying to decipher it. He kept his pedal to the floor and barreled past them, knowing it was too late to think about evasive action.

A glimpse of startled faces swiveled to follow him, and then the Executioner left them in his wake, the dark street clear in front of him. His eyes were on the rearview mirror, watching as the Lincoln growled to life and powered through a U-turn, screeching into hot pursuit of Bolan and his groggy passenger.

Confusion had to count for something, and the gunners would be arguing among themselves by now. If they had glimpsed his face, then they would have to know the Caddy was in strange and hostile hands. And they would pursue him until they made the tag...or until Bolan shook them off his track.

But granting that the gunners might have seen his face, however fleetingly, the Executioner could not afford to merely shake them off. He had to kill them and make damned sure that none of them were left alive to spread his new description.

They would have to die, but not before he had a chance to question one of them, to find out who they were and why they were so interested in his passenger.

The soldier kept his mind on grim survival for the moment, knowing he might never live to extract any intel if hostile gunners overtook him here, in the middle of a sleeping residential neighborhood.

It was not Bolan's way to wage his war with innocent civilians in the cross fire. There were times, of course, when he could not dictate the battlefield, but when a choice existed, Bolan tried to isolate his targets and eliminate the noncombatants from his field of fire.

Like now.

The Continental's driver had recovered from his momentary disadvantage on the starting line, and he was gaining ground, his headlights glaring back like dragon eyes at Bolan from the rearview mirror as the tank bore down on them. The Caddy was already straining near its limit, and the soldier knew he had to try another tactic.

He had made a brief refresher study of the neighborhood before his probe, and Bolan knew the through streets now. He gunned the Caddy through two intersections, finding the one he wanted, finally standing on the brake and cranking hard left on the wheel.

He heard Giamba sliding on the seat behind him, struggling to pull himself erect inside the swerving car. A pudgy hand gripped the back of Bolan's seat, clung briefly, then lost it as he made another screeching turn, doubling back the way he had come. There was a muffled curse as Artie hit the floorboards with a solid thump.

"Goddammit! What the hell...?"

"Stay down!" the soldier cautioned, and there wasn't any time for further dialogue if they were going to survive the next few moments.

On his final screaming turn, the Continental was a full half block behind, and Bolan hoped his sudden deviations from the track had shaken crew and driver. The soldier knew that if he could keep them disoriented, then he had a chance.

The Caddy and its tail were leaving larger homes behind and roaring through the streets of smaller tracts. The warrior marked the vacant lots that opened out on either side, the red light winking on a radio tower away to his left. l The city was behind them now; ahead lay drab industrial developments.

The Continental was a looming silhouette in Bolan's mirror, gaining once again, the driver's confidence returning as his lights picked out the straightway. The tank already had its windows down, and it was bristling with weapons as gunners braced themselves to make a strafing run.

Bolan held the Cadillac at sixty-five and watched the Lincoln closing on his tail, weaving back and forth, the driver seeking room to pass. The soldier held his own tank in the middle of the two-lane road, sharp eyes on the mirror, trying to anticipate the hostile wheelman's moves.

He sprang the AutoMag from leather, and placed it on the seat beside him. He let the Caddy drift off center, giving his assailant room to pass, to try a broadside fusillade. His hand was wrapped around the silver cannon when the wheelman saw the opening and went for it, the Lincoln surging forward like a hungry panther, bright eyes tunneling the darkness.

It was up to the soldier's timing now, split-second expertise that would draw the line between success and failure, life and sudden death. The tiniest mistake would doom him, but Bolan was not ready to concede defeat.

His eyes were on the outside mirror, left hand steady on the wheel, as he tapped his brake and held it for a heartbeat, two, the Caddy instantly responding to his signal, slowing just enough to let the gun crew draw abreast. Another second now, and they would have him in their sights, begin unloading with everything they had at point-blank range.

If Bolan let them have the time.

Big Thunder's silver barrel slid across the windowsill, the Magnum an extension of himself, as the warrior turned to let the gunners have a graveyard smile. Before it had a chance to register, he was squeezing off in rapid-fire and standing on the Caddy's brake, his wagon nosing down to let the Lincoln roll on by at seventy, a gleaming blur with startled faces framed in open windows.

And Bolan's rounds were burning in among them now, exploding window glass and bone, dissolving flesh on impact. Slumped across his steering wheel, the Continental's driver was a twitching rag doll, robbed of voluntary movement by the bullet that had clipped his spine. With no hand upon the helm, the tank swerved left, then right and finally went over in a barrel roll, its four doors flapping and disgorging bodies like projectiles in the night.

Bolan brought his stolen Caddy to a halt uprange, and he was EVA before the Lincoln came to rest, inverted, in the middle of the two-lane highway. Smoke was wafting from the undercarriage, and he knew there would be only moments left before the fuel tank blew, consuming anyone inside.

The AutoMag was empty, and he fed it a replacement magazine as he advanced upon the ruined tank. The soldier marked a crumpled body to his left, another dead ahead and moved on past them. At twenty yards he spied the driver wedged beneath the Lincoln's wheel, the angle of his twisted head and neck testifying to instant death.

Dammit!

He had hoped to take a hostage here, to squeeze some answers in hopes of learning what brought a crew to Art Giamba's fading palace in the middle of the night.

A movement to his right brought Bolan into combat crouch before a wounded gunner showed himself. One arm was clearly broken and a bloody flap of scalp was hanging down across his forehead like a cheap toupee. He dragged one leg behind him, grunting with the pain his effort cost him, straining now to put some ground between himself and the smoldering Continental before it blew.

The hardman's bleary eyes found Bolan almost accidentally, the black-clad image registering slowly on a shell-shocked brain. His injuries retarded the conditioned reflex of defense, but he was digging for the holstered automatic when the Executioner squeezed off one round of thunder at a range of fifteen yards.

A 240-grain shocker cut the gunner's one good leg from under him, and the pistol flew from nerveless fingers as he sprawled facedown upon the pavement. Whimpering, he tried to drag himself across the asphalt to reach the weapon, but the Executioner was there before him, reaching down to pluck the automatic from his fingertips and toss it out of sight.

Bolan crouched beside the wounded gunner, rolled him roughly over on his back so that their eyes could meet. The guy was hurting, and when he drew a breath, the liquid rattle in his throat and chest betrayed internal injuries.

"You're running out of time," the warrior told him bluntly, seeing recognition of the truth behind the hostile eyes. "I need to know who sent you for Giamba."

"Yeah?" The mortuary whisper carried traces of amusement underneath the pain. "Well, you can fuck yourself."

A sudden coughing jag brought blood up from the damaged lungs. The guy was choking on it for a moment, but he finally cleared his throat, and there was grim defiance in his eyes as he regarded Bolan from beneath the fringe of dangling scalp.

"Okay."

The Executioner nodded slowly as he rose, silver AutoMag already sliding out to full extension. The hardman saw it coming, tried to spit at Bolan with his dying breath, but he was short on wind and all he got was another coughing spasm for his trouble.

Bolan sent relief between the bulging, hate-filled eyes, an incandescent mercy burning through to find the brain and cauterize its dark, malignant evil.

Little Art Giamba had regained his seat when Bolan reached the Cadillac, and he was staring wide-eyed at the apparition that slid in behind the steering wheel.

"Holy mother!"

Bolan cranked the Caddy into life again and dropped it into gear, prepared to take them out of there.

"You took 'em all!"

"That's right."

"Do I know you?" the little mafioso asked suspiciously.

The soldier glanced across his shoulder, gave his passenger a look inside the graveyard eyes.

"You tell me, Artie," he replied.

And they were rolling before the mobster had a chance to find his voice, but there was something in the silence that was half an answer in itself. The sudden fear and awe in Artie's eyes had said it all.

3

The mafioso knew Mack Bolan, although he would have been hard pressed to recognize the face. But Art Giamba knew the Executioner, damn right.

They'd called him "Little Artie" since the old days, and the name had been in reference to his five-foot-four physique and not to any shortage of respect within La Cosa Nostra's ruling hierarchy. Back when booze was the outlawed commodity, Giamba ran St. Louis with an iron hand, his tentacles of power reaching across the broad Midwest to strangle competition.

With his childhood friend and lethal ally Jules Pattricia, Little Artie was a power to be reckoned with throughout the heartland of America—indeed as far away as Washington, D.C.

But times had changed and the world rolled over on Giamba in the fifties. He was busted by the Feds and locked away for seven years, while Jules remained behind to mind the store. But he lacked Giamba's business sense, and in the years of Little Artie's exile, raiding parties out of Cleveland and Detroit, Chicago and Miami nibbled at the fringes of a crumbling empire. Returning home, Giamba found his fiefdom withered besieged within the borders of Missouri proper.

Giamba and Pattricia fought to keep their shrunken empire intact against the border raiders from outside. A major headache was New York, where Augie Marinello's appetite had rapidly outgrown his jurisdiction, and the New

York Boss of Bosses mounted endless sorties into Art Giamba's territory to the west. Deprived of all but the most minimal influence on La Commissione, Little Artie dug in for the battle of his life.

And he was on the verge of losing it when Bolan came to town, responding to an urgent flash from Able Team. The New York expeditionary force had taken Artie hostage and was starving him to death before the Executioner arrived to spoil their play.

He had upset the whole equation in St. Louis, leaving Little Artie on his shaky throne as something like the lesser of two evils. In the end, it had not been so much a victory for the Giamba forces as it had been another winning skirmish in Mack Bolan's endless war.

But it was happening again, and so he had returned—not for Giamba's sake, but for his own.

They had ditched the Cadillac, and now the little mobster rode beside Bolan in his rental car. Artie remained silent for a while. They were cruising slowly through a residential neighbourhood before he found his voice again.

"I heard you were alive, but who woulda thought? I mean..."

"I told you I might be back this way."

"I know, but hell...Hey, that's some job on your face. I'll bet your mother wouldn't know ya, huh?"

"My mother's dead."

And the mafioso did not miss the graveyard growl. He shuddered and slid a few inches farther away from Bolan.

There was a momentary silence as they rolled along the tree-lined avenue through early-morning darkness. Artie knew the Bolan story well enough, and he didn't need a fresh reminder of the big guy's own blood debt against the brotherhood. He tried to change the subject.

"Hey, it's lucky that you showed up when you did. Those bastards woulda had me in the bag by now." A sudden thought etched furrows in his brow. "How'd you find out they was gonna hit my place?"

"I didn't know until they pulled up in your drive," he told the mobster honestly.

"So you were coming after me."

His whisper had a desperate, strangled sound within the confines of the car, and the ancient mobster's face took on a pallid look.

The Executioner allowed his eyes to lock with Artie's for a moment.

"I was coming after you to ask some questions. If I wanted more, you wouldn't be alive right now."

A trace of color was returning to the mafioso's thin, anemic cheeks.

"Well, I guess that's right. I never thoughta that. What kinda questions did you have in mind?"

"Let's start with who might want to see you dead."

The mobster's barking laugh was sharp, sardonic. "You got all night?"

"Not even close."

The soldier's tone told Artie more than he had meant to hear, and now he sobered instantly, the bitter laughter dying on his lips.

"I'd say it smells familiar, hey?"

"New York?"

Giamba's shrug was eloquent. "I understand you had a guy up there who called himself a Marinello."

Bolan nodded grimly. "You heard it right, and *had*'s the word. He's dead."

"Could be he died too late."

"Explain."

"It's the same old story, guy. New York gets hungry, and St. Louis feels the bite. This Augie, Jr., or whatever...say he tries to follow in the old man's footsteps an' he wants to cut himself a slice of what we got down here. You with me?"

"So?"

"Le's say he's got some troops already on the way, when he gets wiped back home. Le's say his soldiers think they're big enough and bad enough to carry on without him, hey?

So Augie, Jr. is feedin' worms, an' I still got his army breathin' down my goddamned neck right here, like he was still alive...or maybe worse.''

"Why worse?"

"Jus' think about it, eh? You wiped their boss, his territory's up for grabs back east. So why should these cocks *ever* wanna go back home? They're dead back there. Out here..."

He did not have to finish it. The Executioner was way ahead of him by now, and it made sense. An expeditionary force had been deprived of its commander, and they were fighting now to stake out territory of their own before they were discovered by the rising warlords of their former turf and deemed a threat that had to be eradicated forcibly.

And in a backward sort of way, Giamba's recent plight, all the current trouble in St. Louis, could be traced to Bolan's recent skirmish with the Mob in New York.

One of the Big Apple's rising lights, Don Ernesto Marinello, had turned out to be the bastard son of Augie Marinello, Boss of Bosses and a one-time Bolan nemesis. Resurgence of the Marinello name on La Commissione had been unthinkable to Bolan, and he had been forced to pull out all the stops for one more hellfire cleansing of Manhattan and environs. Underbosses in a dozen gangland families were scrambling to fill the chairs of capos who had fallen in New York, but Bolan had been satisfied to see the hated Marinello name atop his list of casualties.

And now it seemed the name and Marinello's guiding hand were coming back to haunt him in another battlefield. Old Augie's heir was in the ground, but he had set machinery in motion that was running on without him now and which, if Bolan was not careful, might put down roots in the Missouri soil and flourish like some noxious weed.

Giamba's personal security meant nothing to the Executioner. The guy was still a cannibal, but he was a dinosaur, out of place and out of time, approaching personal extinction. And it wasn't Bolan's job to keep the guy in power.

Except that Art Giamba's fall would still create a vacuum, and someone would inevitably be drawn in to fill his shoes. If it was someone after Artie's own convictions, then the operations in St. Louis would go on as they had done for years...some gambling, some ladies who would occupy the time with bored conventioneers, some smuggling and domination of the rural moonshine industry.

But if a Marinello protégé should seize the throne, begin to build an empire along the lines of Don Ernesto's rotten structure in New York...

"I'd say you've got a problem," Bolan told the aging mobster.

"Yeah. So tell me somethin' I don't know already, hey?"

"You have someplace where I can safe you while I take a look around?"

Giamba cut a sidelong glance toward Bolan, chewing on a thought for a while, unable to divine the soldier's motive. "I don't get it, guy. I mean, I'm grateful...This is twice you've saved my ass, but still, it don't add up, ya know?"

The soldier smiled without emotion. "Let's just say I've got a vested interest in making sure New York stays in New York."

Another thoughtful pause. "Okay, I can relate to that...I think. You know Pattricia's place?"

Bolan nodded. "How is old Jules?"

Giamba's voice turned stony in an instant. "Dead, that's how he is. About a week ago. The bastards caught him drivin' home an' put about a hunerd bullets in his car."

Artie's voice was cracking, and the soldier glanced at him, startled by the raw emotion on the little mobster's face. Giamba and Pattricia had gone back some forty years together, and clearly there had been a bond between them that was more than surface deep.

Giamba got himself together and continued as the soldier cut a U-turn, homing in on Jules Pattricia's neighborhood.

"Jules had a boy. Name's Bobby. Anyway, he's livin' out there now an' takin' care of business. Jus' like his old man, I tell ya that. A goddamn rock.''

The voice was running out of steam again, and Bolan let it go, continuing the drive in silence. He had battle plans to make, and there would be more time for talking when he dropped Giamba at the old Pattricia place. With any luck, he might meet Bob the Rock, and get a better feel for what was coming down in Artie's camp.

He might be able to enlist an ally, although his better instincts warned him to stay clear of any tie-in with the Mob.

There was a lot he had to learn about the New York expeditionary force, before the Executioner went public with his war.

He had already taken out almost a dozen of the outside guns. It would be good to let them chew on that for a while, wondering where ancient Artie found the muscle to respond with such ferocity to their surprise attack. In time, they would come looking for the answers.

And Bolan would be waiting for them, bet on it.

To welcome them with open arms.

*Fire*arms.

4

Gray dawn was spreading rumpled wings across St. Louis, but around the old Giamba mansion it was almost noonday bright. The red and blue strobe flashes from patrol cars, ambulances and fire trucks were reflected off the crumbling facade of Artie's palace, and their high-beam headlights brought the shadowed grounds alive.

They could not do the same, however, for the sheet-draped figures lined up on the gravel driveway. One of them had already been stowed inside the wagon; six more were waiting patiently to join him now, with no damned hurry in the world.

Capt. Tom Postum, head of intelligence for St. Louis PD, surveyed the carnage with an expert's eye, his face impassive in the artificial glare. Beside him, a lieutenant from the orgcrime unit was examining the burned-out Cadillac.

"No sign of Artie?" Postum asked.

"Nothing yet. He's one of those that fried."

Tom Postum shook his head. "He won't be. All of these were in the hit team, unless I miss my guess. We know Giamba didn't have a hard force on the grounds."

The lieutenant looked puzzled. "So where is he then? And who laid out this crew?"

Postum shrugged. "The old man didn't do it all himself," he said reflectively. "I'd say some help arrived before these cocks could do their thing."

"Pattricia?"

Another shrug. "It's worth a look. Find out where Bobby was tonight, and where his boys were, if you can."

"No sweat."

"We'll need to make these cars, for what it's worth."

"They'll all be rentals."

"Yeah, but let's go through the motions anyway."

"You read Scarpato into this, Cap'n?"

"Any better ideas?"

"None that make any sense."

The young lieutenant waited while a team of paramedics placed another sheeted form inside the ambulance.

"Man, I've never seen anything like this. Have you?"

Tom Postum glanced at the lieutenant, nodding slowly. "Once or twice."

And the captain from intelligence had seen it all, and not so long ago. Then, two Mob factions had declared war in his town, each determined to eliminate the other. And someone had intruded on the battlefield to even up the odds, to pull old Art Giamba's sizzling fat out of the fire.

Mack Bolan.

So yes Postum had seen this before, in spades.

Sometimes he even saw it in his dreams.

With close to twenty years in the department, he was recognized as both a seasoned veteran and member of the tough "new breed."

The savages were keeping pace with current trends and new technology, and it required a grim new breed of cop to deal with them. Tom Postum and a team of others like him were determined that the future of the Mafia around St. Louis would not be a rosy one. They had been putting pressure on the Mob, applying their strategic heat with surgical precision since the Bolan blowout some years back. They had been making inroads, too, and scoring gains.

But lately, it seemed to Postum as if the world was reversing on its axis, carrying him back to the bad old days. Another shooting war was brewing in his streets and he was right back where he started when the Executioner had come to town.

No, scratch that. He was worse off than before, with all the changes in the Mafia that he had witnessed through the past six months. Giamba was the same old codger he had always been, with one foot in the grave and the other on a banana peel. But Jules Pattricia, his one-time heir apparent, had been cut down first, and now his son, young Bobby, was on standby with his soldiers, waiting to step in if Artie fell.

That meant another generation of the old Giamba family in St. Louis, providing they could hold on to their territory and their lives another week, another month.

The SLPD captain worried just as much about New York, the soldiers who had turned up on his turf and who were raising hell right now, attempting to unseat Giamba in what had the earmarks of a bloody insurrection. Rumbles from Manhattan told Postum that the spearhead was without a headshed now, but if it cramped their style at all, it wasn't showing yet. If anything, Scarpato and his men were stepping up their raids, increasing pressure on Giamba to fight or flee.

The thought of Vince Scarpato made the captain scowl. He had already interviewed the New York transplant twice, arrested him on more than one occasion for offenses that were bargained down to nothing in the lower courts. It was harassment, and Postum made no bones about it under questioning from his superiors. His goal was to evict the New York raiding party from St. Louis, and so far Postum was batting a perfect zero.

A thought struck Postum, and he suddenly felt dirty. A traitor to his uniform.

The captain had been close to wishing Bolan back, and never mind the hell the soldier had raised around St. Louis, the bodies he had left for Postum to clean up when he was through...

But dammit all, the guy got results and Postum knew what made the soldier tick...at least, he knew the story of his family, the tragedy that had claimed their lives...and still, he wondered how the dude had carried on so long, alone.

There had been mixed emotions in St. Louis when reports of Bolan's death came in from Central Park. The politicians and the brass downtown had been relieved, but there were rumblings among the street cops, that the country needed someone who would take the soldier's place, and soon.

It was a feeling Postum knew too well, and one he fought against from day to day. He knew that Bolan's way was "wrong," according to whichever book you chose, and yet...

The bastard got results.

The captain had been home, relaxing on a rare day off, when news of Bolan's "resurrection" reached him via television. Shock had jostled with confusion in his mind, but there had been a flash of something else.

Elation.

He had been *glad* to hear the Executioner was still alive and tearing ass, but that awareness made the lawman in him react with an instinctive guilt to the tacit "betrayal" of his oath.

And he could rationalize a part of it, of course. The hellfire guy had saved his life last time around, extracting Postum from a burning vehicle before the fuel tank blew them both away. He owed the soldier one.

The captain sometimes wondered how he would react if faced with Bolan now.

It worried Postum that no ready answer came to mind.

He shrugged it off, aware that he would do whatever was required of him to keep the lid on in St. Louis. At the moment, it was Art Giamba and Scarpato's men who were the problem.

Mack Bolan wasn't in St. Louis.

The captain turned back in the direction of the burned-out Cadillac and the sheet-draped forms.

Artie had no hard force at the house. Postum would have known if the old mafioso was going hard, importing troops.

The obvious solution was that Pattricia had somehow found out about the raid, sent a rescue force to pull his capo out of there before it was too late. It would have given Bobby one more chance to even up the score for his old man while he was at it.

"I want ballistics on this yesterday," the captain told his sidekick. "We need to know how many different guns it took to do all this, their calibers, what blew the Caddy over there..."

"You got it, Cap."

"I want a tail on both Scarpato and Pattricia, around the clock. Don't make it any secret, either. If we need more men, you let me know."

"There shouldn't be a problem after this."

The captain nodded, frowning. There was nothing like a public massacre for shaking loose the reinforcements a commander needed. Nothing like it, either, for producing heat to close the case before the public started howling in administrative ears.

Tom Postum didn't mind the heat as long as he was free to work a case his way and bring it to a close without a crowd of second-guessers getting in his way.

A uniformed sergeant was approaching, his stride determined, face grim. When he was within earshot he hailed Postum, drawing his attention from the gutted Continental with its line of bodies in the foreground.

"Call for you, Captain. Looks as if you've got another one."

"Another what?" Postum asked, the crawling sensation along his spine the only answer that he needed then and there.

"Another one of these," the sergeant answered, sweeping a big hand across the killing ground. "Four down so far, and counting."

"I'll be right there."

The sergeant nodded, backtracked swiftly toward the cruiser with the message.

"Sounds like Scarpato's got a *real* war on his hands," the young lieutenant said. "I guess old Artie's not the jelly roll we thought he was."

"Don't underestimate the bastard," Postum cautioned. "He was fighting for these streets when you were still a twinkle in your daddy's eye."

There was a hesitance about his tone, and the lieutenant sensed it, picking up on the vibrations. "But?"

"But nothing. Maybe it just doesn't *feel* right."

"Well, sir...if it's not Giamba..."

"Yeah, who could it be?"

He trailed the beefy sergeant back in the direction of the cruisers, knowing that he had a long damn day ahead of him, for sure. With four more down at yet another shooting scene, it would be noon before he finished with the lab crews and pathologists, the newsmen and the paramedics.

He didn't like the feel of this one. Not at all. And it was more than just the thought of one more street war in St. Louis, all the wasted time and wasted lives. The captain had a city ready to explode, and he was sitting on the lid, doing his damndest to keep it in place. So far, his record of success was nothing to write home about.

He needed time to think it out, to find out what was eating at his insides. But his time was running out, Postum knew, along with everybody else's in the orgcrime intelligence unit. If they let this thing blow up in their faces, if they were unable to prevent—or at least predict—the next grisly outbreak of violence, then certain people would inevitably start to "reassess" their function.

Postum had devoted too much time to building up the unit to see it all go down the drain, and he was determined to stay on top of the developing war in his town. If that meant taking to the battlefield himself, so be it.

And it was starting to look like the old days. In spades. For half a second there, before he reached the cruiser and the radio, he almost wished it was the old days again.

But they would have to do it all themselves this time, without a hellfire warrior to step in and do the dirty work on their behalf. This time they would be forced to do it on their own.

Tom Postum wondered, for the first time in his memory, if he was equal to the task.

5

Giamba phoned ahead from an all-night convenience store, alerting his new underboss to what had happened in the past two hours. Pattricia would be waiting for them both when they arrived...and that gave Bolan second thoughts about his hoped-for meeting with the younger mafioso.

He was running short on time already, a stop at Bob Pattricia's now would put Bolan even further behind in a race in which he was already trailing.

Add to that the risk of walking into hostile territory where he would be instantly surrounded, with no backup support and small hope of escape if it soured.

In the end, he opted for unloading Artie in the next block up from Bob Pattricia's hardsite mansion. Before the soldier pulled away, he had Pattricia's private number firmly in his mind, along with Artie's reticent agreement to provide him with intelligence as it became available.

And he was gambling, the warrior knew, when it came down to trusting any mafioso, anytime. Giamba would have killed him in an instant if it had been to his advantage. But Bolan had a notion that the aging mobster would be looking for allies, and that he would be glad of one more gun—especially Bolan's—to bolster his failing ranks.

The Executioner had no intention of allowing his crusade to be divered into some kind of bizarre Giamba rescue mission. He was in St. Louis to destroy the savages, and Little Artie would be ranked among the first to go if he betrayed the soldier's trust in any way.

But for the moment, there were other targets, other problems, on the hellfire warrior's mind.

The battlefield was chillingly familiar to him, as so many others were the second time around.

The hostile sides were still the same—or nearly so—and any superficial changes in the names and faces of his enemies did not concern the Executioner.

The cleansing fire strategically applied, and let them fry if they weren't fast enough to find their rabbit holes before the flames descended to consume them in their tracks.

But if the killing ground and Bolan's enemies were still the same, what of the stakes? Exactly what was riding on the line this time in old St. Louis?

Bolan shook his head and cursed the lack of battlefield intelligence that dogged his movements in the river city. What was the equation that had inspired another bold invasion from the east?

Little Artie had grown weaker since Bolan had last been here—there was no doubt of that. What remained of his territory must have appeared like easy pickings to a cannibal of Ernie Marinello's appetite.

But there was more at stake than annexation of St. Louis to the New York orbit. The soldier had a feeling that the rumbles pointed to the founding of a whole new family—rapacious, strong—that would replace Giamba's creaky structure with a sleek and lethal war machine.

Before he dropped Giamba off, the Executioner had learned the name of Little Artie's New York nemesis: one Vince Scarpato. He led the expeditionary force for Marinello...but Scarpato was his own man now, cut loose from his foundations in Manhattan, rootless, with nothing left to lose.

The name was not unknown to Bolan, though his mental mug files had no detailed background on the guy. He had begun his tour of duty as a button man in the Bronx, performing dirty work for this or that regime until he fell within the Marinello jurdisdiction and was drafted into service. His reputation was replete with violence—murder, arson, rape, felonious assault—and he was leadership material within the brotherhood of blood.

A cannibal, in need of Bolan's personal attention, sure.

But not just yet.

The soldier would do everything within his power to prevent the founding of another family in old St. Louis. He would spend his last drop of blood, if that was what it took to get the job done right. But he was not about to throw his life away on some fool's errand, charging blindly into hostile guns.

Bolan's war was not about St. Louis, or New York, or any other single battlefield along the way. It was a universal struggle with universal stakes, and he could not afford to blow it all for the sake of getting finished quickly.

And it was still the same old war, beneath the superficial changes, sure.

Good versus Evil.

Civilization versus the Savages.

Right.

It was the longest-running war on record, and it showed no sign of burning out, in Bolan's lifetime, anyway. His struggle had predated history, and it would certainly survive the passage of a single hellfire warrior. His dying, when it came, would hardly make a ripple, but he could damn well make some ripples while he had the chance.

The Executioner could make some tidal waves, for sure, and sweep some savages away before his clock ran down. St. Louis was ripe for such an action, overdue, in fact, but first he had to have a better handle on his war.

And Bolan's tactics would remain the same. He would cling tenaciously to training that had carried him this far along the hellfire trail. It was the difference in his personal approach that kept his enemies off balance, and it never crossed his mind to change a winning style.

Bolan fought his war in stages, each defined and clearly separate from the others, though civilians might have failed to comprehend the difference.

Precision made it mandatory that he should *identify* the enemy before he struck, eliminating tragic errors and cutting off escape of stragglers or guilty front men masquerading as beleaguered innocents.

After singling out his targets, Bolan sought a way to *isolate* them in the killing ground, preventing law-enforcement officers and stray civilians from being drawn into the line of fire.

That done, he used the full range of his martial skills to finally *annihilate* his foe, allowing no one to escape the cleansing fire. His war was to the death. He also knew that the death would someday be his own. But Bolan took his own destruction as a foregone fact of life, and lived each day as if it were his last. He would be living large until they cut him down in battle. And with the stark reality of personal destruction came a liberation from the bonds of doubt and fear that hobbled other soldiers. There is no man so totally efficient, the warrior knew, none so dangerous, as one who does not fear to die.

And Bolan was such a man.

It was said that he had been hardened in the crucible of Vietnam, in his war against the Mafia and in his Phoenix phase, but such was not the case. In Nam, where he had earned the Executioner tag, Mack Bolan also had been known as Sergeant Mercy. More than once the Man from Blood had risked his life under fire to retrieve injured comrades and wounded civilians and had seen them safely back inside the friendly lines.

And caring had driven him along the grim attrition road of his own private, endless war. What had begun in rage, a quest for vengeance in his own backyard, had grown into a war against injustice, evil and oppression of the weak, anywhere and everywhere beneath the sun.

He fought because he could, because he had to, sure. It was his duty to correct the wrongs he saw around him, to expunge the evil that imperiled decent men and women in their daily lives. He could no more desert his post than he could give up breathing voluntarily.

The Executioner was in for the duration, yeah.

Identify.

Isolate.

Annihilate.

It was search and destroy, just like Nam. Just like Pittsfield.

Just like always.

But he would need some intel on the local scene, and Little Artie had had sparse information. It could be that the aging mafioso knew no more than he had said, or that for reasons of his own, he had been holding something back.

No matter.

Either way he had provided Bolan with a glimpse inside the maze, and there were other ways to map its many corridors.

The soldier had some other sources of battlefield intelligence, all ready at his fingertips in time of need.

One source of information was as close to Bolan as the nearest telephone. He only had to drop a dime and tap into the reservoir of knowledge that was waiting for him at the other end.

The other source would cost him more, in terms of risk and danger, but it might pay off with all the answers necessary to complete phase one of his campaign.

If he was cautious and did not overplay his hand.

If nothing unforeseen arose to take him on his blind side.

If he could make it through the first lap intact. Alive.

The phone call first, before he risked it all on one roll of the dice. He needed something more to go on before he put his head into the hungry lion's mouth.

And Bolan could already feel the hot breath on his neck. It raised the small hairs, made them tingle with apprehension, warning of peril close at hand.

It felt like danger.

And it smelled like death.

6

The filling station had seen better days. Its pumps were cobweb covered, and the shelves inside the building were stripped of anything that might invite a thief. A faded cardboard sign, hung crookedly on the inside of the plate-glass door, proclaimed it Closed Til Farther Notis.

Someone had forgotten to remove the pay phone tucked at the rear, and Bolan parked his rental back there, alert to any sign of danger as he stepped inside the dusty booth.

He dropped some coins into the slot and punched up a long-distance number from memory. Allowing for the difference in times, his contact should have been awake, or even sitting down to breakfast now. The soldier waited patiently through half a dozen rings until the deep, familiar voice came on the line.

"Hello?"

"Long distance for La Mancha."

"Uh...he isn't in right now. You got a number there so he can call you back?"

He read the pay phone's number slowly, waited while it was repeated to him and broke the connection.

In Baltimore his contact would be grumbling about the early-morning hour, but preparing all the same to go out and return the call, as arranged in their established code. It would require some time for him to reach a safe phone, far enough from home to guarantee the line was secure, but Bolan could afford to wait.

His contact was a mobster named Nino Tattaglia, a "made man" in the Mafia with years of street experience behind him. In his early thirties, Nino was an up-and-coming lieutenant in the family of Don Carlos Nazarione, the East Coast's grand old man.

It had begun for Nino with a murder bust that would have meant the end of his career, his life outside of prison walls. Hip deep in the assassination plot, he took a look around and realized he had only one choice, really. So he "turned," becoming an informant in exchange for guaranteed immunity from prosecution. Anytime that someone on Hal Brognola's staff could spot a lie in his covert reports, they merely had to dust the old indictment off and pick up with the game where they had left it—one step short of trial and sentencing. There was no statute of limitations on murder, and Tattaglia was theirs, damn right, as long as they had need of him.

He had replaced a dedicated infiltrator, Leo Turrin, who was a "first" for Justice in his day, their only man within the inner councils of the Mob. When Turrin had revealed himself, providing epic testimony in a string of trials, then quietly submerging into Bolan's Phoenix Team, to fight the terrorist wars beside his oldest, closest friend, it had been vital for Brognola to secure a functioning replacement in the ranks as soon as possible.

And then came Nino.

But he was more, in Bolan's mind, than just a "stoolie," bought and paid for with a bargain made in judge's chambers. At first Bolan had been skeptical of opening his business up to someone he had never seen or heard of before—and someone who was raised inside the hostile camp, at that. But time had proved Tattaglia to Bolan's satisfaction.

Like the fact that Nino still provided him with solid information despite the fact that Bolan had become a renegade, completely severed from the workings of the Stony Man and Justice teams.

And like the fact that Nino clearly was uneasy now with some of the arrangements other mafiosi had been making on their own, the power plays and politics of murder tucked away behind the scenes. He had begun to show compassion and there was nothing in his secret contract with the government that forced the guy to *care*.

It had to come from *inside*, and Bolan was impressed.

Impressed enough to put his life in Nino's hands each time he dropped a dime and made a call to Baltimore. The little mobster could have turned him in at any time these past few months, collecting rich rewards from both of his employers—government and Mafia—but he had kept their secret locked away inside himself, and he was still available, when Bolan needed battlefield intelligence about the inner workings of the Mob.

A quarter hour passed before the pay phone rang, and Bolan did not let it have a second chance.

"La Mancha."

"Hey, I guess that makes me Sancho, huh?"

The mafioso's voice was shrunk by long distance, but his sense of humor came through loud and clear.

"So how's the action on the river?" Nino asked, attempting to sound casual.

"It's heating up. I need to get a solid handle on what's happening."

"Uh-huh."

A hesitation on the other end, as Nino pulled his thoughts together, running through the memory banks for useful information on St. Louis. Bolan waited patiently through almost a minute of dead air before the husky voice filled his ear again.

"You know Giamba?"

"Well enough. He owes me one. I've got a shaky line inside his house."

"That's good…except the top brass at La Commissione aren't talking to him much these days."

"Is he cut off?"

"It's not official, but they've got a lot of other problems cooking now, you know? Long Island left a lot of families without a man on top, and they've been scrambling like mad to fill the vacancies. I hear that California's trying to secede."

Long Island was the site of a recent Bolan blitz against the Mafia, and he had wiped no fewer than a dozen dons, along with Augie Marinello's bastard son and heir. That kind of vacuum at the top created chaos in the Mafia until each family found a strong man to assert control and bring the drifting troops back into line.

"I wish them luck," the soldier told his friend. "All bad."

"You just might get your wish. So anyway, the families who lost somebody at Long Island are tied up right now, and some of them are starting to look sideways at the bosses who weren't there."

"Like Artie?"

"Bingo."

"Last I heard, he wasn't even asked."

"So true. But you're still thinking logically, all right? I'm talking *paranoid*."

"Okay. Go on."

"So maybe no one thinks Giamba set it up. He hasn't had that kind of weight behind him now for years. But still, they don't quite trust the guy, ya know? He wasn't big with La Commissione before the shit came down on Marinello's head, and now..."

"What have you got on Vince Scarpato?" Bolan asked.

"A Marinello soldier. Anyway, he *was*. Word is, Ernesto sent him west to do a little midnight annexation for the family, you follow? Only you took out Ernesto, and now Vince is like a guy without a country."

"How does he stand with other families?"

"They haven't started blaming him for anything, so far," Tattaglia replied. "Right now, the heat's divided up between yourself and Don Ernesto's memory. As far as Vincent goes, they're playing Wait and See."

"What happens if he manages to put down roots?"

"Well, that depends. He's got the Marinello taint right now, but if he found himself a territory far enough away and let things cool awhile...who knows? It may be months before they have a voting quorum at the headshed, anyway. A lot of things can happen in that time."

"So there's a chance that he could be confirmed." Bolan felt the pieces beginning to fall in place.

"Why not? If he can make some friends, convince them that he's not a threat to anybody, sure. They wouldn't miss Giamba—you can bet on that. Most of them never met him, anyway. They're not real big on strolls down memory lane these days."

"Nobody wants Scarpato then?"

"Not as far as I know."

"Does *he* know that?"

Another heartbeat's hesitation, as Tattaglia read the meaning behind Bolan's words. "I'd say he's guessing now, like everybody else," the inside man replied. "He should be pretty nervous, what with his communication and supply lines cut the way they are."

And Bolan knew he had his handle.

He only had to get a grip and turn it, open the latch.

Tattaglia seemed to read his thoughts. "You plan on going inside this one, guy?"

"I thought about it."

"Watch Scarpato, eh? He's razor sharp, they tell me. And he's not alone."

"I'm counting on it," Bolan told his friend.

"Just so you know. And don't put too much faith in Artie, either. He's a fossil. Bob Pattricia's the engine in that Model T."

"I'll make a note."

Bolan thanked his contact and hung up swiftly retracing his steps to the rental car.

The soldier was looking forward to his meeting with the razor-sharp Scarpato. If the guy was operating on his own, as Nino had said, then logic told the Executioner that Scarpato would be running short of money, weapons, men.

And time.

The clock was running down on Marinello's expeditionary force. Each passing day would bring them closer to resolving the chaos that was gripping La Commissione, and that much closer to the possibility of intervention by another hungry family, which could field more troops, more guns. The longer Vince Scarpato stalled, the smaller chances for a victory became, and any soldier worth his salt would have to recognize that fact.

It was the kind of pressure that leads to paranoia, to mistakes. The kind of situation where the Executioner could work, providing he was smooth and fast enough to pull it all together in a strangler's knot around Scarpato's neck. If he could make his way *inside*...

And it was risky, but that had always been the name of Bolan's lethal game. He knew the odds against him going in, and he had played those odds before.

"He's not alone."

Tattaglia's words came back to Bolan now, reminding him that he was up against a hostile army once again, one that had already lost perhaps a dozen soldiers in its first engagement with the Executioner.

Scarpato would be wondering, by now, what had gone wrong with his attack upon Giamba's palace.

The mobster from Manhattan would not have the troops to waste, and every man he lost was one more strike against him. He could not do the job alone, and if he failed, there would be no place left to go, nowhere to hide.

Scarpato would be wondering how Little Artie had repelled his strike force. He would be questioning his own security, looking for a leak, a traitor in the ranks.

It was time for Bolan to take full advantage of Scarpato's paranoia. He might not have a better chance than this again.

A chance to foil Scarpato's plans for empire in St. Louis.

A chance to guarantee, at least for now, that there would be no drastic changes in the river city Mafia.

A chance, perhaps, to die, if he made a single slip along the way.

The odds were long, but the stakes were too damned high for him to let the opportunity slip past. He had to seize the time and make his living moments count while they remained.

The Executioner had never shied away from risk, from danger, and he was not starting now. The action lay with Vince Scarpato, in the hostile camp, and the doomsday warrior was going where the action was, carrying the fire.

He would be living large until he died, and if the moment came today, then he would give it up and pass the torch to the other hands.

Mack Bolan would keep fighting in the only way he knew, against the cannibals and savages who preyed upon the decent people of the world.

And he was going where the action was.

Inside.

7

The gate man was in uniform, as if he might have been on duty at a country club instead of on a middle-ranking hit man's payroll. All spit and polish topped with cool efficiency, he did not raise an eyebrow as the sleek red Vette nosed into Vince Scarpato's driveway.

The gate man had not seen his face before, and so he took his time about approaching the Corvette, consulting his clipboard as he eyed the license tag suspiciously, making a show of his mundane routine.

The sportster's driver was a hardman, by his looks. Expensive threads could not conceal his muscular, athletic build, and there was confidence, determination in the face. And the gate man was certain that the mirthless smile the stranger wore did not reach the eyes, invisible behind mirrored sunglasses.

"Can I help you, sir?"

The guard's tone was distant, cautious, as he gave the man behind the wheel a second look.

"I'll bet you can," the driver answered, frozen smile in place. "I need to see Scarpato. Like, right now."

Another riffle through the clipboard's sheaf of papers. Nothing matched the date and time.

"Are you expected, sir?"

"I hope not."

And the gate man was still puzzling over that one when the driver of the Vette produced a laminated card, extending it in one big, manicured hand.

It was an ace of spades.

The sentry swallowed hard, thought better of examining the clipboard once again. He held the death card gingerly between two fingers, studying its mute design, and finally passed it back as if afraid it might transmit some lethal germ through contact with his flesh.

"I ought to call the house," he said.

The driver's smile was slipping. Going...going...gone.

"So call."

The cordial tone had left his voice. It blew across the gate man's nerves now like a graveyard breeze and set his teeth on edge.

"Well...no, I guess that won't be necessary," he decided, stepping back a pace from the Corvette. "Just let me get the gates."

Bolan watched the gatekeeper's back as he retreated toward the little sentry hut and stepped inside, one nervous index finger jabbing at a button that controlled the gates. Another moment and the broad gates started rattling and creaking open, riding on their hidden tracks.

He drove through without a second glance in the direction of the guard. The guy might well have second thoughts, announce him to the house in spite of his original decision but it didn't matter either way. Not now.

He was inside, and there was nothing left to do but play the cards that he had drawn, whichever way they fell. By passing through those gates he had consigned his fate into the hands of Chance.

Role camouflage had been a Bolan speciality since Vietnam, when he had learned firsthand that human beings do not always see what may be placed before their eyes. The mind was part of visual perception, too, with all its preconceived ideas and expectations. It could color and distort what people "saw" until the physical reality was lost, illusion in control.

By putting on an attitude, a set of clothes, Bolan could become a member of the hostile camp, and they accepted him as if he were another cannibal invited to the feast.

The anonymity surrounding the Black Aces, the Mafia's one-time gestapo, assisted Bolan in his penetrations of the Mob. The Aces changed their names, their appearances to suit the occasion. Within the Mob, this elite corps spoke for La Commissione directly, and their word would often pass unquestioned, even by the ranking dons.

It was too good a situation to resist, and he had used it more than once. But each time he put on the Omega mask, each time he showed the death card, Bolan risked exposure as a fraud. And there could only be one penalty to fit the crime.

A death as slow and agonizing as his enemies, collectively, were able to devise.

The risks were even greater now, he knew, with the Ace's ranks dwindling, in general disfavor with a number of the bosses coast to coast. A real Black Ace might very well be treated to the same reception as Bolan if the Ace turned up in the middle of a family intent on staking out a future of its own.

The sword could cut both ways, damn right...but at the moment it was all he had. And he would take the risks, without allowing premonitions of disaster to distract him from the task at hand.

He powered the Corvette along one hundred fifty yards of curving driveway, finally arriving at the mansion that Scarpato had selected as his base of operations in St. Louis. Once the home of an eccentric oil tycoon, the place had gone to seed, but it was still maintained with more attention to detail than Art Giamba's aging west-side palace.

Bolan marked the floodlights mounted at the corners of the second floor. Closed-circuit television cameras focused on him as he parked the Vette out front, not far from carbon-copy Cadillacs.

And he had seen their mates last night, at Little Artie's. He had been driving one of them when he dispatched the hit team's backup gunners. If Vince had brought a fleet of them along with him from New York, his stock was being whittled down.

The massive front doors opened, and a houseman sidled out to meet Bolan as he reached the marble steps. The gunner's jacket was unbuttoned, and he kept one hand pressed flat against his abdomen as if enduring a bout of heartburn, watching **Bolan** with a hunter's eyes, alert for any move that would provide him with a cause for hauling out the hardware.

The death card was in Bolan's hand before he reached the doorman, its solitary spade resembling a fat black widow spider perched upon his fingertips. The houseman took one look at it and lost his heartburn, gun hand sliding down until it rested limply against his thigh.

"We weren't expecting you," he said.

"That's right."

The gunner hesitated, finally dredging up his voice from somewhere deep inside.

"This way, sir."

Bolan followed through a lavish entryway, with sunken parlors opening off either side, along a corridor decked out with tapestries and stylish reproduction prints. The gunner led him to a well-stocked library and left him with the promise that Scarpato would be down to join him shortly.

He was in, and that was half the battle. The other half was getting out alive—but not until he had accomplished his objective. He had come here to assess the enemy and leave a little something of himself behind.

Like doubt.

Disunity.

Dissenion.

Already bloodied in their first engagement, Bolan's enemies were ripe for some subversion from within.

Bolan took a look around the library while he waited, scanning shelves of leather-bound volumes that extended to the ceiling. Strategically positioned chairs were all mahogany and leather, placed to take advantage of the light from massive windows that comprised the western wall.

The door behind him opened softly, and he turned to face his host. A decade older than his latest mug shot, Vince Scarpato had been softening around the middle, but nothing of the softness showed through in his eyes. He looked the new arrival over, frowning, and did not extend his hand.

"I don't know you," the mafioso said.

"No reason that you should."

A flicker, deep behind the eyes, of something dark and dangerous.

"The doorman didn't catch your name."

"I didn't throw it, Vince. You can call me Omega."

"Uh-huh." Suspicion simmered in his voice. "What brings you out this way?"

"We heard you had some trouble on your hands."

"That right? Who's we?"

The Executioner ignored his question pointedly, continuing as if the mobster had not spoken.

"Could be you made a bad mistake last night."

Scarpato raised an eyebrow, feigning ignorance.

"I guess I just don't follow you," he said.

"That move on Little Artie, Vince. You nearly blew it."

"Yeah?" Defiance was competing now with curiosity, and running second best. "So how's he doin', eh? He coulda come an' told me that himself."

"He's busy, Vince. Been on the phone all morning. You know how it is."

Defiance stumbled, lost on the inside curve.

"I didn't know he had so many friends," Scarpato said.

"You'd be surprised. A lotta people still remember how it used to be. The good old days, ya know? A lotta people hate to see times change."

"That kinda thinking killed the dinosaurs."

"Could be this dinosaur's still got some life left in him, Vince. Could be he's not alone."

"You say."

"I haven't said a thing," the Executioner replied. "If it comes down to that, I haven't even been here, Vince."

"Okay. So what about those calls?"

"Long distance, man. You've heard of that. They've got a phone line now goes all the way back east." Scarpato smoldered, but he held his tongue as Bolan forged ahead. "I hear some people in New York were getting wake-up calls today."

"So what's that mean to me?"

"The phone lines run both ways, Vince. Airplanes, too."

"I got a lotta friends around New York," Scarpato said, his tone defensive now despite his brave facade.

"That so? Well, shit, no problem then. I guess I just misunderstood about the changes that were going on back east. I mean, they woulda told you all about it, right?"

"I guess."

"I guess. Who'd want a piece of your ass, anyway? I mean, they all must know how loyal you were to Ernie, right?"

No answer, but the mafioso's face had paled beneath the sunlamp tan, and he was thinking fast now, toting up his friends and enemies inside his skull.

"I guess I had it all ass-backward, Vince," the Executioner went on. "I mean, it just makes sense that any friend of Marinello's is a friend of yours."

And Vince was thinking that one through, racking his brain for the name of a friend in New York and coming up empty, when the door behind him opened unexpectedly. The mobster jumped involuntarily, eyes narrowed as he turned to face the new arrival.

He was tall and lean, well-groomed, athletic looking in his flashy suit. Gray eyes swept past Scarpato, locking on the mirrored pools of Bolan's shades.

"What is it, Stone?"

The new arrival closed the door behind him, took another stride into the room.

"I heard we had some company. A VIP. Just thought I'd say hello."

The tone was almost condescending, and Scarpato glowered, first at the intruder, then at Bolan, finally turning back to face the man called Stone.

"You prob'ly know him as it is," Scarpato growled. "He's one of yours."

"That so?"

Stone cocked an eyebrow, took another casual stride toward Bolan, and alarms were going off inside the soldier's head now, raising gooseflesh on his arms and urging him to get the hell away from there.

"They call me Stone," the gray-eyed gunner told him through a plastic smile. "And you're..."

"Omega."

The hardman's frown was contemplative as he tried to remember the name.

"Can't say I've heard of you, but what the hell..." His tone was frosted with a thin veneer of ice. "I guess you wouldn't mind me checking out your hole card."

Bolan had a heartbeat to decide if he should bolt or play the gunner's game. The laminated ace was in his hand before his thoughts had time to take on conscious form. The gunner scrutinized it closely, finally turned to pin Scarpato with a glare.

"You look at this?"

The New York mobster shook his head suspiciously.

"They cleared him at the gate."

The gunner handed Bolan's calling card to Vince Scarpato, turning back to face the Executioner directly.

"Bullshit, Vince. It's bogus as the day is long. You've got a ringer on your hands, you poor dumb—"

Bolan did not let him finish. From a standing start he threw himself at Stone, the heel of one hand slamming into the gunner's chin. It was a killing blow, but Stone had seen it coming soon enough to save himself, step backward slightly, and instead of suffering a broken neck, the guy was lifted off his feet, propelled directly into jarring contact with his capo.

Stone and Scarpato sprawled together on the floor, all thrashing arms and kicking legs. The soldier could have taken them, right there, but he was in survival mode and focused on escape, intact, from what had suddenly become a most unhealthy atmosphere. And for every heartbeat he delayed his exit now, the odds against survival lengthened geometrically.

The warrier left his adversaries wrestling with one another, cursing, kicking, as he sprinted for the west wall with its bank of windows. It was chancy but at the moment it was all he had.

And Bolan leaped, eyes closed, arms up and crossed to shield his face from the explosive impact as he hit the glass dead center, plunging on and through.

He hit the flagstones in a fetal curl and kept on rolling, shattered glass cascading down around him. It snagged his clothing, cut him, but the soldier closed his mind to pain, his focus on the grim totality of life and death.

Behind him in the study, Stone and Scarpato were already on their feet, the Black Ace hauling hardware out from undercover, sighting in on Bolan's wobbling, rolling form. A bullet pocked the flagstone inches from his face, and now he had the sleek Beretta in his fist, already pivoting and coming upright in a combat crouch, returning fire.

The gunner, Stone, had seen it coming, and he dodged behind a leather-covered easy chair, his parting shot so high and wild that Bolan didn't even have to duck. The soldier picked out Scarpato, already scrambling out of sight and out of range before he fixed the target in his mind, and Bolan began to move, his destination the Corvette.

Inside Scarpato's rented house, the gunners would be scrambling. Some of them would be in the study now, as

Bolan cleared a corner of the house and started pounding toward the driveway.

How many guns?

How many cannibals arrayed against him here on hostile turf?

He realized that numbers did not matter now. It would only take one lucky shot to bring him down and end it all. And all the odds were on Scarpato's side this time.

A shout behind him, dangerously close, and he was twisting, going over in a diving shoulder roll before he heard the gunshots. Angry hornets sliced the air above him as he flattened on the ground, bringing the Beretta up and into target acquisition.

Two men, out of breath from unaccustomed running, and he caught them both flat-footed now, their weapons still directed toward the point where he had been a heartbeat earlier. Before his swift evasive move could register, he was already sighting down the autoloader's slide, squeezing off a deadly double punch at less than twenty yards.

The taller of the two gunners staggered, sat down hard, his stainless .45 forgotten as he brough both hands up to his throat. A ragged vent had opened there, spraying frothy blood across his white dress shirt. From fifty feet the Executioner could hear him wheezing, struggling for breath and losing it, the life light burning out behind his eyes as he collapsed back on the grass.

His partner tried a sidestep and he almost made it. Almost. The second parabellum sizzler drilled his cheekbone underneath an eye, and kept on reaming through to make explosive exit just behind the other ear. The guy was staggering another pace or two while his muscles took their last commands from dying brain cells.

Bolan did not wait to see the walking zombie fall. The warrior was already up and moving, still homing on the flame-red shark that was his one last hope of clearing the Scarpato grounds alive.

He made the final corner, running free and clear, the hot breath scalding lungs and larynx as he pushed himself beyond the limit. Another eighty yards and he would reach the sportster, slide behind the wheel....

And they had reached the red Corvette before him.

8

A squad of hardmen, two or three with shotguns in their hands, circled the sports car, bending to peer through tinted windows, tugging at the doors in vain. As Bolan pulled up short another clutch of gunners exited the house, two of them moving toward the Vette, the others peeling off to either side at double time, intent on circling the house to search him out.

It took perhaps a heartbeat for the nearest hood to spot him, shout a warning to the others as he swung an M-1 carbine up and onto target with instinctive speed. And Bolan knew that it was over even as he stroked the sleek Beretta's trigger, dropping the rifleman before he had a chance to fire a shot.

The other guns had seen him now, and it was now-or-never time.

Already prone as they began unloading on him, the soldier slid one hand inside his jacket, found the little detonator clipped inside his belt, above one hip. He keyed the single button, held his breath and hugged the lawn as doomsday came among them with a vengeance.

At a range of eighty yards the sportster reared, its front tires rising, followed by the rear, and it was levitating on an oily ball of flame. It took another fraction of a second for the thunderclap to reach him, and Bolan rode it out with eyes closed and face nuzzling the turf.

A secondary blast destroyed the Vette before it settled back to earth. The air was thick with shrapnel—twisted steel, splintered glass, and the shattered fiberglass. A ghastly rain was falling over Bolan now, the heavens drizzling shredded flesh and weeping crimson for the hardmen who had stood too near the sportster when she blew.

The Executioner was on his feet and moving, scanning for survivors, as the sanguinary shower died away. He glanced in the direction of the house where windows had been shattered by the blast, and he found the open doorway momentarily empty. They were lying low in there, still trying to decipher what in hell was going on, or else the other troops had found themselves in a different exit, fanning out across the grounds to search for him in other quarters.

Either way, the blast would bring them running soon, and Bolan had no time to spare. He heard the doomsday numbers falling in his mind, and he was looking for an alternative escape route when a flaming scarecrow lurched erect beside the ruins of the Vette, his arms a smoking windmill as he screamed his life away through blistered vocal chords. A silent mercy round reached out to clip the dancing puppet's strings, and he collapsed beside the crackling skeleton of Bolan's wheels.

Around him other dazed survivors were beginning to recover something of their wits. The nearest of them was already on his feet, shaking his head and dabbing at the blood from ragged scalp wounds dripping into his eyes. When vision cleared he saw the smoking ruin of the Vette, half turned, and found the Executioner regarding him from less than twenty paces out.

The gunner's first reaction was professional and smooth, considering the circumstances. Digging for his gun, the minor wounds forgotten now, he reached his belly holster in a single fluid motion...and he found it empty.

Realizing he had had the weapon in his hand before the world fell in, the gunner cast around in desperation, searching for it at his feet. The eyes that locked with Bolan's were afraid and angry at once. They registered the bitter knowledge of defeat. And Bolan sealed that knowledge for eternity with an explosive round between those eyes.

Another pair of guns were on their feet to Bolan's left now, and he swiveled to confront them. Both had clung to weapons when the shock waves mowed them down, and they were clinging to them now, the deadly muzzles winking flame and tracking onto target acquisition.

Bolan never let them get there. Squeezing off in rapid fire, he caught the nearest gunner with a double punch through heart and lung, the impact blowing him away. Then Bolan swiveled to concentrate on the dying hardman's comrade, the Beretta chugging in his fist.

And number two was staggering, the life already running out of him through twin holes in his chest. He made a gurgling sound, expelled a crimson bubble from his throat and toppled slowly foward to the blood-stained grass.

The Executioner was running overtime, his numbers gone. He spied the line of Caddies still in place, the closest to his shattered Vette already smoldering, and sprinted for them as a shouted warning from the porch alerted him to new arrivals on the scene.

He gambled that Scarpato's men would feel secure enough inside the grounds to let their guard down, kiss off some of the security precautions that are second nature to a full-time warrior. Ducking behind the nearest Cadillac, he found the driver's door and wrenched it open, slid behind the wheel and found the key still dangling from the ignition.

He cranked it over, careful not to flood the engine as he worked the pedal with his foot, aware of soldiers closing on his flank, already plinking at the car. The Cadillac was taking hits, a Magnum round exploding through the small side window at his back, but now he had the engine revving and he dropped the monster into gear, releasing the brake and smoking rubber in reverse.

Behind him, gunners scattered as the tank bore down upon them, veering in a wicked fishtail skid that caught one pistolero unaware. Before the hardguy had a chance to avoid the hurtling tank, the fender caught him square and dropped him in his tracks, his torso half beneath the rolling juggernaut.

Bolan felt the Caddy lurch, ignored it as he ripped the lever into Drive and jammed the pedal to the floor. His tires lost traction briefly, spinning in the human stew, and then they found the pavement once again, screeching out of there with force enough to jam the warrior back against his seat.

A dazed survivor of the Corvette blast staggered into Bolan's path, the Diamondback revolver anything but steady in his bloody hands. There was no time for evasive action as the Caddy hurtled toward him, accelerating into lethal impact, lifting him and rolling him across the broad expanse of hood. Screaming face met windshield glass with stunning force, a crimson spiderweb of cracks erupting from the point of impact, and the gunner clung there for a moment, staring lifelessly at Bolan through the fractured glass, before he slipped away and disappeared across the fender.

Concentrated pistol fire followed the Caddy, peppering its tail and shattering the broad rear window, spending lethal force inside the trunk or in the cushions of the deep back seat. The warrior risked a backward glance and saw the dwindling gunners as they scrambled for remaining cars, intent on giving chase.

And he was watching in the rearview mirror as it went to hell.

The burning Cadillac exploded, spewing gasoline and oil in fiery streamers, touching off a dozen secondary fires among the other cars in line. The gunners scattered, dodging shrapnel, beating at their clothing where the flames had taken hold.

There would be no pursuit in those machines, but Bolan could not take a chance that Vince Scarpato had other wheels at his disposal. The warrior was still inside the dragon's turf, outnumbered and outgunned. No time for letting down his guard or easing off on the accelerator yet, not with the hounds still baying at his wheels.

It was becoming something of a habit, borrowing the opposition's wheels for an impromptu getaway. A risky habit, one that he would have to break if he intended to pursue his everlasting war by means of anything resembling coherent strategy.

The time for playing it by ear was past, and he would need a more dynamic plan of action to carry off the action in St. Louis.

If he was able to escape from Vince Scarpato's armed estate intact.

If he did not encounter fatal opposition at the gates, which were his only means of exit now.

Two hundred yards, and Bolan knew they would be waiting for him, right. It was a question of how many men, how many guns, the fear they were willing to endure to bring him down.

He was banking on that fear, and counting on the mercenary guns to flinch from death when it was thrown directly in their faces.

One hundred yards and he could see them now, a clutch of gunners fanning out to block the exit with their bodies, weapons drawn and angling onto target. Bolan spied the gate man in his spit-and-polish uniform, a chrome revolver braced in both hands, in the classic target shooter's stance.

At fifty yards they opened fire, and Bolan ducked beneath the dashboard, keeping pressure on the gas, the steering wheel rock steady in his hands. He heard the hornets smacking into grill and bodywork, the sudden steamy hissing of a punctured radiator and the windshield detonated into pebbled fragments, littering the dash and floorboards.

At twenty yards the hardmen scattered, all but one of them in time to save themselves. The gate man stood his ground dead center in the Caddy's path, still squeezing off in rapid fire, the hammer falling now on empty chambers. Bolan straightened in time for impact, and he met the dead man's eyes with less than half a second to spare.

The Cadillac struck man and gates together, forced his body through the wrought-iron grillwork like tomatoes through a kitchen grinder. The force of the collision threw Bolan forward, bruised his chest against the steering wheel, and then the gates gave way, their relatively fragile structure bending, twisting outward underneath the crew wagon's momentum.

Bolan clenched his teeth against the rending, grating sound of ironwork being dragged along the Caddy's length on either side. It threatened to hold him for an instant, finally surrendering to the power of his V-8 mill. Then the tank rammed through and he was free.

For now.

Until a roving traffic cop or spotter for the syndicate got one look at his battered, bullet-punctured wheels.

The Caddy's dashboard was ablaze with warning lights, alerting him to engine damage, shortages of water, oil and gasoline. The radiator was expelling plumes of steam, and he could smell escaping coolant through the open dashboard vents.

The tank was dying on him and he would have to ditch it.

Before Scarpato and his watchdog, Stone, could mount a new pursuit.

Before the wounded Caddy gave up on its own and left him stranded in the open, easy prey for those in pursuit.

There was a chance that he could make it to the "safe" garage where he had stashed the other rental car, but it was just a chance, no more, and he would have to sacrifice the drop.

So be it.

Bolan held the pedal down and concentrated on the road—ahead, behind, to either side.

There was no safety for him now, he knew, in St. Louis, but the thought did not deter him from his chosen course. There was no safety in St. Louis for Scarpato, either. No safe haven for the man called Stone.

Not while the Executioner survived.

He was alive and for the moment, that was all that counted. Bolan's enemies would soon be hearing from him once again.

9

It had been too close for comfort, for damn sure.

The Executioner's precaution, wiring up the Vette for doomsday on the chance that he might need a desperate diversion, was enough to save him...this time. But he could not count on luck to see him through this mission in St. Louis.

Bolan was a cautious warrior, trusting more in strategy and preparation than in chance. He knew the value of reconnaissance and never trusted a simple fortune if he had a choice. He had survived his lonely war so far because he never trusted anything except himself, his weapons and his will to win.

The warrior who began to think himself invincible was quickly and invariably proven wrong, he knew from grim experience. And there were no immortals in the hellgrounds.

Next time out, the Executioner would have to try a different tack to reach Scarpato in his lair. Next time they met, the Man from Blood would not be after information.

He would be coming for Scarpato's head, to crush the serpent's brain beneath his heel and see the final spark of life snuffed out before his eyes. And Bolan knew that nothing less would be required to see the battle for St. Louis through.

He was disturbed by Stone, Scarpato's watchdog, and the ease with which the Ace had seen through his Omega mask. It raised a host of questions, and none of them were meant to put the soldier's mind at ease.

It bothered Bolan that Stone had marked his calling card as bogus...not so much because it almost cost the Executioner his life, as that the card, in fact, was genuine. He had retrieved it from the body of a fallen Ace in one of his engagements with the Mafia so long ago, and it had served him well.

Until today.

But Stone's reaction to the card was puzzling, disturbing. There had been something in the laminated pasteboard that had sounded an alarm inside the gunner's head, betrayed Bolan to his enemies.

And so far he had no idea exactly what that "something" was.

The card itself was back inside Scarpato's study, and he did not have another to compare it with. There must have been some change in the design, the calling card itself, that had alerted Stone to Bolan's scheme.

The answer sent a chill along Bolan's spine. New calling cards would mean new Aces. A second coming of the Mafia's gestapo, possibly regrouping in the service of another would-be Boss of Bosses somewhere up the line.

But when had they begun reorganizing?

How?

And why?

The Aces were a breed apart, a law unto themselves within the brotherhood. Conceived as the elite enforcement arm of La Commissione, they had at one time carried the authority to hit a capo on their own initiative, as long as they could justify it later to the ruling board. It was an awesome power in itself, and only one of several that the Aces used to keep themselves on top, the black knights of an evil kingdom, serving the not-so-round table of the nation's ranking mafiosi.

When Bolan had launched his one-man war against the syndicate, the Talifero brothers had been running things at Black Ace Central, taking orders only from the headshed in New York. Identical twins, Pat and Mike had been as ruthless as they came in the underworld jungles, two killing machines devoid of conscience. They ruled the roost by the fear that they inspired, and of the New York bosses only Augie Marinello had had the grit to give them orders on his own.

The Bolan challenge had been a natural for Pat and Mike. They very nearly tagged him in Miami, and again in Vegas, but each time he had left them licking ragged wounds.

It had been Bolan who discovered that the Aces were the brainchild of old Barney Matilda, Marinello's right-hand man from Prohibition days. The Talifero brothers were Matilda's sons, and before the Executioner finished off his second mile against the Mafia, he had made a clean sweep of the family. He took out Marinello for good measure, settling another ancient debt, and he had been convinced that the surviving Aces were a dying breed.

Until recently, that is.

A foul new wind had risen in the East, and Bolan had pursued it to its source, surprised to find the Marinello name ascendant once again around Manhattan. Augie's bastard son had tired of waiting for his father's throne, and he was moving in to take it when the Executioner arrived to spoil his best-laid plans. A dozen dons had fallen in the bloodbath on Long Island, spreading chaos through the underworld, but once again Bolan had been left with a bitter taste in his mouth.

For there had been an Ace named Lazarus at Marinello's side. And Bolan was thinking now of Lazarus. Of Stone.

The Aces chose their street names for effect. Matilda's vicious sons, the Talifero twins, had picked a name that aptly mean "such iron." And Bolan's choice—Omega—spelled the end, for any cannibal who crossed his path.

But Lazarus...

Perversely, members of the Mafia had shown a penchant for extracting codes and cover names from holy writ, as if the lifting of a phrase from scripture could ensure success for some unholy enterprise. Barney Matilda himself had been code-named Peter.

And what of Lazarus?

The guy had risen from the dead all right, but briefly, and the Executioner had sent him back again to stay.

Now Stone.

Another Peter?

Was the goddamned guy a new foundation for the Mafia's gestapo? Was he more than just an adjunct to Scarpato's orphaned expeditionary force?

Reviewing his encounter with the mafiosi, Bolan thought that Stone displayed a healthy dose of cheek to Vince Scarpato for a simple gunner on the payroll. Not that any Ace was ever "simple," but at the same time, few would ever call their would-be capo stupid to his face. But Stone might be something more than what he seemed, and Bolan could not well afford to underestimate the Ace, especially if he had a resurrected crew of Mafia assassins at his back.

The scattered Aces, drifting randomly like plague bacilli on the wind, were bad enough. Regrouped into a fighting unit once again with leadership in able hands, they would be nothing less than catastrophic.

Revival of the Aces meant negation of a major victory for Bolan in his war against the Mafia. It meant reversal of the inroads he had made against the syndicate, a rude about-face to the bad old days when capos coast to coast had known the power of a swift, efficient army at their beck and call.

It was a grim concession to the enemy that he was not prepared to make.

Not while he lived.

The Executioner had lately risked his life, the lives of friends, to cauterize the Marinello cancer. He had believed that it was finished, finally, in New York...and now he understood that he had only been ensnared by wishful thinking.

It was never finished as long as Bolan's enemies survived, all breeding in the shadows, spreading, a writhing mass of inhumanity.

He would take them as they came, as they revealed themselves and stood to face his righteous wrath. He would erase them, foundations and all, at every opportunity.

Right now he had unfinished business in St. Louis, yeah. It went beyond Giamba and Pattricia, beyond Scarpato, reaching to the very origins, the root of Bolan's private holy war. It was a primal need that drove him now, compelled him to remain and wage relentless war against the cannibals.

Scarpato.

Stone.

He realized that names meant nothing in the final scheme of things. The changing names and faces, the alliances and old antagonisms, were as transient as the shifting desert sands.

The only constant for Bolan was his war.

The need to fight.

Because he could.

And in the last analysis, it mattered not if Vince Scarpato sought to found an empire for himself or for some other don who hid behind the scenes and pulled his strings.

Ernie Marinello was dead, and Scarapato had survived him, carried on his taint, his evil work. Scarpato had become a Marinello, in soul if not in name. Precisely as the gunner, Stone, had now become a Lazarus, a Talifero clone.

The enemy was nameless, faceless. He was timeless, sure, like Bolan's everlasting war.

The enemy was here.

The Executioner could see his duty clearly, and he knew precisely what he had to do.

Wipe out the Marinello taint.

Eradicate the Aces, no matter what their current numbers were.

Keep hammering the Mafia, because it *was*. Because he owed it to the thousands of forgotten victims. The women, tricked or trapped into a life of hopeless degradation and sold like cattle. The ruined families, whose names the Executioner would never even know.

The warrior owed them all, but not because of anything that he had done himself. He owed them because he had the raw ability to wreak a fearful vengeance on the cannibals.

The soldier fought for all of those who never found the strength to stand against the common enemy.

It was a thankless war, at times. An everlasting war, for sure.

And Bolan knew that his "second mile" against the Mafia had not been finished on that rainy afternoon in Central Park, when he allowed himself to "die" and was "reborn" again as Colonel John Phoenix. The mafiosi had been with him then, and they were with him still.

Still the same.

Still deadly.

Still the enemy.

His bloody trek through hell would be completed—part of it, at any rate—when he had killed them all. When there were no more new recruits to take their places in the ranks.

It was a damned tall order, but Bolan knew that he was up to it.

Or was he?

Never mind.

He focused on the here and now and let the future fret about itself. He would be living through that future soon enough, providing that he lived at all beyond St. Louis.

Here and now was all that mattered to the Executioner. It was the only grim reality he had.

And it was high time to teach the savages a lesson in the only language they could understand. If he survived, there would be other times and other lessons. Other enemies.

If he did not, then he would take as many of the bastards with him as he could, oh yeah. And they would know that he had been there.

The Executioner would give them something special in the way of a forget-me-not.

Like hell, perhaps.

Delivered to their very doorsteps.
Gift wrapped.
With a blood-red bow.

10

The neighborhood's shady streets were lined with trees and houses set on spacious lots, each home an individual design without the cookie-cutter feel of less expensive tracts. There were no mansions here, but you could fairly smell the subtle elegance that characterized a bastion of the upper crust.

Behind the curtained windows with their burglar bars, the doors with triple dead bolts polished bright like a combat decorations, St. Louis's professionals were safe to carry on their ordered lives. It was a nighborhood of doctors, dentists, lawyers, ranking merchants. Here, a city councilman, perhaps, and there, a captain of police who found the wherewithal to live beyond his salary. In style.

Bolan drove along the quiet boulevards, observing traffic regulations, nodding at the private uniformed patrolman who passed by him in the opposite lane. His rental car would fit the neighborhood—just barely—and any casual observer would dismiss him out of hand. He would be "someone from the office," visiting a business partner or associate to talk about their common problems over brunch.

A casual observer would not make the Beretta autoloader slung beneath his arm, the silver AutoMag beneath the rental's dash in spring-loaded leather. A passerby would not suspect the other military hardware hidden in the trunk—enough of it, in fact, to make the quiet residential street a bleeding war zone if the Executioner desired.

The soldier was not hunting now, but he was searching. Behind his mirrored shades, the narrowed eyes were scanning housefronts, curbs and picking out the numbers. Another block, no more, and he would have the house he sought.

A drive by showed him two cars parked outside, and Bolan had his quarry now. He had already phoned downtown, to be informed by an indignant secretary that his contact would be out today. All day. The house had been a last resort, but it was paying off.

He cut a cautious U-turn in the middle of the block and doubled back to park the rental curbside, out in front. There was no point in looking for an alley or attempting to conceal the car. In such a neighborhood, evasive movements would have drawn attention. The best way to conceal himself, he knew, was to be as obvious as hell and act as if he came here every day.

He had not called ahead this time, preferring to surprise his quarry, catch him with his guard down.

He locked the car and left it, striking off across the broad expanse of lawn to circumvent a winding concrete walkway. He risked a final backward glance along the street and punched the door bell.

Inside the house, melodic chimes were tolling, and he missed the sound of footsteps drawing nearer, muffled by expensive deep shag carpeting. Alerted by the racket of the dead bolt, he was ready when the door swung open...but he was not quite prepared for what he saw inside.

Chuck Newman looked as if a dozen years and more had passed since Bolan's last visit to St. Louis. But time alone could not explain the shadows underneath his eyes, the worry lines etched around his mouth. One hand was out of sight behind the door, his other tightly clenched against his side, as if in anger...or to keep the hand from trembling.

He was looking Bolan over with a mixture of suspicion and impatience written on his face. When Newman spoke, his voice was tight and brittle. "Can I help you?" he inquired.

"Could be," the Executioner replied as he removed the mirrored shades. "And then again, there may be something I can do for you."

It was the voice, in combination with the yes, that finally put it all together for him, and the prosecutor let his fist relax, a measure of the tension leaking out of him at last.

"My God."

"Not even close."

The guy remembered where they were and cut a glance over Bolan's shoulder toward the empty street, alert to any sign of prying eyes. When he was satisfied he stepped aside and beckoned Bolan in. The door clicked shut behind him and the dead bolt rattled home with grim finality.

"You caught me by surprise just now," the one-time politician told him, almost managing a sheepish smile. "I never thought…"

He let it trail away, as if completion of the sentence was a pointless waste of energy, and motioned for the Executioner to follow him. A moment later they emerged into a sunken family room and found a woman waiting seated on the couch. At the sight of Bolan she was on her feet, the fingers of her hands entwined and held before her in a desperate, almost prayerful attitude. Bolan recognized the prosecutor's wife, the feverish anxiety they seemed to share like a family trait.

"My wife," Chuck Newman said by way of introduction. As he spoke, he shook his head in a dejected negative and she went limp, almost collapsing back upon the cushions of the couch.

"Who are you, then?"

Her voice was balanced on the edge of tears, and Bolan felt as if he had been dropped into the middle of a conversation. Newman did not speak, but he was watching Bolan now, uncertain what it might be safe to tell his wife about this man, this warrior who had turned up on their doorstep unexpectedly.

The Executioner resolved it for him, opting for the truth.

"The name is Bolan," he informed her. "You can call me Mack."

Astonished recognition flickered behind the red-rimmed eyes, and he could almost hear the silent questions jostling around inside the lady's mind.

She was a beauty despite the tears, the harried look, and he could see why she had cherished hope in younger days of a career on stage and screen. He understood how looks and youthful innocence had gotten her in trouble, led her through the back door of the movie business into sleazy porno features touted by producers as a "stepping-stone" to Hollywood, the Big Time. It had been a stepping-stone to nowhere, and Bolan knew how that worked, too.

The soldier put old business out of mind and took the chair Chuck Newman indicated with a nod. The state's attorney found a place beside his lady on the couch. A spring-steel silence hung between them momentarily, and Bolan gave them time to find their way around it gingerly. Chuck Newman was the first to break the ice.

"We were expecting someone else just now," he said. "That is, I thought..." He hesitated, swallowed hard and tried again. "We got a call this morning, early. I was on my way to work.... I almost didn't answer it. My God..."

The prosecutor brought his hands up, covering his face, and Bolan waited. When the moment passed Chuck Newman seemed determined to proceed.

"Our daughter, Bonnie," Newman said, and Bolan felt the hackles rising on his neck. "They have her. She's been kidnapped."

"Who are they?"

"No names, of course," the prosecutor told him bitterly. "But it's Scarpato. I'm convinced of it."

"Why so?"

"The caller made certain demands. Oh, he left all the details to me, but the gist of it was open season on Artie

Giamba, Bobby Pattricia...every goddamned hood in town, except Scarpato's crew.''

''That's tidy.''

''Sure. My office does the mop-up for him, clears the way, and Vince steps in to fill the vacuum. We get Bonnie back when it's done...signed, sealed and delivered.''

''You don't believe that,'' Bolan told him. It was not a question.

''No. I don't.''

Beside him on the sofa, Newman's wife was wrestling with panic, barely holding on. This new exchange between the men appeared to galvanize her, and she clutched her husband's arm now, taloned fingers digging deep into his jacket sleeve.

''What do you mean? *What are you saying?*''

Bolan took the question, fielded it while Newman disengaged himself and slid an arm around the lady's shoulders, trying desperately to comfort her.

''Vince Scarpato has a hole card now,'' he said. ''If it pays off, he'll raise the stakes until he has it all. He can't afford to lose his new advantage right away. He can't afford a witness who could tie him to a federal charge.''

''I understand,'' the lady told him, and there was a trace of steel beneath the tremulous voice. ''You're saying that he has to kill our daughter now, whichever way it goes.''

''Eventually,'' the soldier answered, ''yes. That doesn't mean we're helpless, though. There may be time to turn this thing around.'' He faced Newman squarely. ''What's your deadline?''

Newman drew a ragged breath, released it slowly through clenched teeth. His eyes were hollow, windows on a soul grown numb from too much pain.

''The caller said twelve hours. If I haven't moved against Giamba or Pattricia by tonight...''

He left it hanging there, unfinished, and the soldier knew the rest of it, damn right. The threats and implications of the penalty for failure to cooperate, perhaps with certain grisly details added from the caller's own imagination. For kicks.

It turned the soldier's stomach, but he was accustomed to a war devoid of rules. The savages were acting predictably, and if ferocity comprised their strength, predictability might prove to be their fatal weakness, damn right.

"Twelve hours then," he told the grieving parents. "Give me ten of them, and let me see what I can do. If I don't have your daughter back by...let's say five o'clock...you'll still have time to start a sweep, take some of Artie's people off the street for openers."

The lady's eyes were darting back and forth from Bolan to her husband now, but Newman's gaze was riveted upon the Executioner.

"What can you do?" he asked.

The soldier frowned.

"You've seen me work before."

"This is my daughter, guy. Not some scandal. Not my goddamned fly-by-night career. This is her *life*."

And Bolan felt their pain, in spades. The Sergeant Mercy part of him was deeply touched. The Executioner inside him wanted action, swift revenge against the animals who had produced this sick assault on a decent family.

"Your daughter is at risk right now," he told them both. "I won't do anything to stretch her odds. Scarpato knows I'm here...or will, before the morning's out. He won't connect the two in time to save himself."

"But now—" Mrs. Newman began.

Chuck Newman interrupted, edging out the query from his wife.

"We would be gambling with our only child," he said.

"You've lost her as it is," the warrior told him bluntly. "If you play it by Scarpato's rules, she's gone for good. You know that."

Newman nodded slowly, woodenly. "Ten hours."

"Maybe less. And I'll need to see a photo."

"Okay."

Beside him on the sofa, Newman's wife was silent, huddled within the yielding cushions like a child intent on blocking out reality. Then the distraught woman reached for a framed eight-by-ten that was sitting on an end table next to the couch. She reluctantly extended the picture to Bolan, as if releasing it would somehow shatter any hope of seeing her daughter again.

Bolan saw the tears that glistened on the lady's pallid cheeks, and they were real. As real as heartbreak, agony and death.

He committed the photographic image to memory, then stood, and the prosecutor rose to show him out. They remained above the woman for an instant, watching her, the husband's heart in tatters and the soldier's going stony cold.

Someone was going to pay for all this needless pain, and warrior Bolan was already totting up the tab.

It bore Scarpato's name, and Stone's, together with a crew of bad John Does he had already marked for execution in his mind. It was a start.

Chuck Newman saw him to the door and stepped outside ahead of Bolan, scanning, finally satisfied the street held no surprises for his guest. They stood together on the threshold for a moment, and the prosecutor held Bolan with his probing gaze.

"Do you believe she has a chance?" he asked.

"I do. If I can get to her in time."

"I started this." Chuck Newman's tone was ripe with self-reproach. "If I had done my job...if I had never called..."

"You're wrong," the soldier told him flatly. "Vince Scarpato is a cannibal. He would have come around to this eventually. If not today, next week. If not your daughter, someone else's."

Newman wasn't buying it, but he was able to approximate a weary smile.

"Okay. And thanks...for everything."

"Hang on to that. I haven't finished yet."

He left the prosecutor standing there and put that house of pain behind him, moving briskly toward the rental car. His mind was racing into confrontation with the new and unexpected problem that had fallen in his lap.

The Executioner had come to Newman's home in search of answers, and he was coming out again with brand-new questions, brand-new risks to complicate his private war. Except that it was no longer private, damn right. The enemy had added innocent civilians to the pot, and it would be his task to sift them out again before the mixture reached a rolling boil.

He felt a certain regret for lying to the Newmans, telling them Scarpato was incapable of adding two and two. Whatever Bolan did from here on out, he would be risking Bonnie Newman's life at every step. At the first mistake, he would have her blood on his soul.

It was already crowded there, and Bolan needed no reminder of the missing allies, of the screaming "turkeys" scattered back along his hellfire trail. So many wasted souls. So many lives snuffed out on his account.

And this one, sure, would be all his, as well. The soldier knew his intervention in St. Louis had provoked Scarpato to this desperate action, forced his hand by leveling the shaky odds between Giamba and New York. If he had stayed away, gone about his business somewhere else, they might have killed each other off without involving innocents along the way.

Except, he knew, it didn't work like that in grim reality.

Giamba had been losing when the Executioner stepped in, and when he fell, when Bob Pattricia's die-hard troops had been exhausted in the field, Scarpato and his crony, Stone, would be the reigning bosses of St. Louis and environs. It would be a new day for the river-city syndicate, and life would never be the same again.

The innocents, Bolan knew, had been involved from the beginning of his war, and they would be involved until the final shot was fired and died away. They were his war, his purpose, sure, and he could not have served them here by stepping out and letting Scarpato have his way. He might be risking Bonnie Newman's life by any move he made against the Eastern strike force now, but there was no alternative in Bolan's view. It would be worse if he did nothing, let her waste away and die a prisoner in the Scarpato camp, because he feared to take a chance.

And if she died because of him, because of Scarpato's hunger for territory, there would be hell to pay. Scorched earth for all concerned, and never mind the private cost to Bolan's body, to his soul.

He was prepared to bring the city down if Bonnie Newman was harmed in any way, and if he had to spend his own life in the process...well, the Executioner had been prepared for that from the beginning of his war.

It was a risk he lived with every waking hour of every day.

It was a grim, recurring dream that dogged his sleep and brought him to each dawn with knowledge that it might well be his last.

The Executioner could not undo the pain Scarpato had inflicted here, but there was something he could do to stop it in its tracks. If sacrifices were required he had a list in mind, and Bolan's name was up there with the rest.

The deathwatch in St. Louis was beginning.

There was no way in hell of knowing who would live to see another dawn, and Bolan realized it didn't matter anymore.

This day was all that mattered, here and now.

This day would make or break Scarpato's fortunes...and the Executioner's...in old St. Louis.

Bolan had ten hours to kill, and the irony of that thought did not escape him as the numbers ran down inside his head. Already precious moments were slipping through his fingers like so many grains of sand.

The sand—and time—ran out.

For Bolan.

For Scarpato.

For St. Louis.

It was Zero Hour, minus ten and counting. Beyond that deadline, Bolan could not see a thing.

He kissed tomorrow off and put the war machine in motion, drawing energy, assurance, from the rhythm of its meshing gears. The Executioner was home again, in hell, and he was going to make it hot for all concerned.

11

Tom Postum pushed back his swivel chair, raised his feet and rested them across the corner of his desk. Through heavy-lidded eyes he watched distractedly as the smoke from his cigar collected near the ceiling fixture.

But his mind was on the streets, and on the war that was becoming grim reality around his city. Doctors at the county morgue were working overtime with better than a dozen corpses piled up. There would be other customers before the day was out, he knew, and knowing it produced a sour taste in Postum's mouth.

He didn't like the waiting while others did the legwork, but there was nothing more that he could do himself. As he was leader of the city's strike force, it was his job to lead, and that meant Postum had to make himself accessible to his detectives in the field. He could not always lead the charge himself. He had to delegate responsibility and dabble grudgingly in all the office politics that kept a modern law-enforcement agency in motion.

Slow motion, Postum thought disgustedly, his hooded eyes pursuing yet another smoky plume in the direction of the ceiling. He was primed for action and at the same time, he was dreading it. For action meant more blood, more bodies in the streets, and he had seen enough of that in more than twenty years behind the badge to last a dozen lifetimes.

This new explosion was the worst that he had seen since, well, since Bolan. His mind kept coming back to that, the hellfire hours—had it really only been a single day—when a single dedicated man had run a breakneck race with death. And won.

Tom Postum didn't like to think about those days. They brought back other memories, of Postum's closest brush with death in more than twenty years of facing off against the savages. And whenever he remembered, he felt claustrophobic closeness of the capsized black-and-white. He smelled the leaking gasoline, heard the crackle of a hot wire sparking into life and knew that it was over.

And then he heard the voice.

From somewhere overhead, reaching through the fog of pain and fear to snap him out of it and make him lift his head, his hand.

He heard Mack Bolan's voice, and saw those graveyard eyes above the soot-smudged cheeks, a flash of ivory in the heartbeat smile.

Tom Postum owed the guy his life, and knowing it diminished him somehow. Perhaps because Bolan had been—dammit, was—the nation's number-one most wanted fugitive. Perhaps because the captain had not collared Bolan when he had the chance.

Perhaps—and he had to admit it—because there had not been a chance to pay back the soldier.

The telephone beside Postum jangled shrilly and he picked it up on the second ring. His eyes were on the ceiling and his mind a thousand miles away as he wedged the instrument against his shoulder, answered absentmindedly.

"Intelligence—Captain Postum."

"I thought you'd be commissioner by now."

His daydream and reality collided with a grinding, grating sound that brought the strike-force chief erect, his heels impacting on linoleum with jarring force.

"Too damned much politics," he said, amazed that he could speak at all.

"Good choice."

He recognized the voice at once, beyond the whisper of a doubt. His memory was better than a voice-print analyzer when it came to this one, and he would have staked his reputation—hell, his pension—on his first impression.

Bolan.

Speaking to him on the phone. From where?

The captain knew before he spoke, and still he had to test the certainty. He had to prove it to himself.

"Is this long distance?"

"Strictly local," Bolan answered, and the captain felt his stomach going over in a sluggish barrel roll.

"Okay."

"You've got a problem in your city, Captain."

"Yeah. I think I'm talking to it now."

"So think again. The New York delegation's getting hungry. Someone needs to bring them into line."

"I'm working on it," Postum told him gruffly.

"You could use some help."

"No thanks. It's covered," Postum lied.

"I didn't spot your men this morning," Bolan said. "They must be good."

"So that was you?"

"I had a piece of it. Scarpato called the tune."

"Uh-huh. You wouldn't know where I could find a certain capo, would you?"

"Artie's safe and sound, for now. You've got a more important problem on your hands."

"Oh, yeah? What's that?"

And Postum listened as the Executioner explained about the Newman girl and Vince Scarpato. As Bolan spoke, the strike-force captain felt his insides churning slowly and alarms were going off inside his head.

"He should have come to me," Postum said when Bolan finished speaking.

"Right. And have Scarpato waste the girl as soon as he finds out police are on the case."

"You think you've got a better chance of springing her?"

"Damn right. I won't be going in with one hand tied behind my back."

The captain ground out his stogie with vicious, stabbing thrusts against the plastic ashtray, knuckles white and bony where he gripped the telephone with grim intensity. He knew the goddamned guy was right, but he could not admit it to himself, not openly.

"We don't need any vigilantes in this town," he said, and knew it sounded lame before the echo of the words had died away.

"You don't need any murdered women, either, Captain."

"Yeah. Okay. So why tell me your plans?"

"I haven't told you anything," the soldier countered smoothly. "That would make you an accessory."

"All right." The weariness was evident in Postum's voice.

"Scarpato's cut himself a slice of hell on earth," Bolan said, the deep voice suddenly intense. "I don't want any blue suits getting burned."

"I don't want anybody getting burned," the captain retorted, but he knew it was a lie before he spoke.

He wouldn't mind Scarpato getting toasted in the least, and that went for his gunners, too. If Art Giamba's crowd should get smoked out along the way, so much the better in Postum's eyes.

But it was *wrong*, and he could not allow himself to sanction Bolan's extralegal plans through silence any more than he could actively assist the man in black.

"The town's on fire already," Bolan told him. "Maybe you should let it run its course."

"You think so?"

"Fire gets rid of vermin, Tom. It clears the air."

A part of Postum wanted to agree with Bolan, but he shrugged it off, rocked forward in his swivel chair, both elbows resting on his desk.

"I can't help thinking someone might object if I sat back and let you stoke the furnace by yourself."

"I didn't start your brushfire, Captain," Bolan told him. "But I'm smart enough to know it can be channeled, used."

"I'm not a forest ranger," Postum told him sourly. "I've got a job to do, and if you hang around St. Louis you're a part of it."

"All right. Now we understand each other."

Postom swallowed. Was that a trace of sadness in the soldier's voice?

"Now we do," the strike-force captain mumbled.

"Good luck."

The line went dead before he could reply, and Postum found himself alone again inside the tiny office, suddenly deprived of Bolan's presence that had filled the room a heartbeat earlier. The nagging dial tone grated on his nerves, and Postum slammed down the receiver, rocked back in his swivel chair again to ponder the soldier's final words.

"Good luck."

"You, too," he told the emptiness, surprised and then embarrassed by the sudden tightness in his throat. "You too."

ART GIAMBA WAS TIRED of hiding out and jumping at the smallest unexpected sound.

Of running like a frightened rabbit on his own home ground.

Of acting like the hunted, when he should have been the hunter, standing on his own two feet and fighting back.

It made him sick, this sitting in a shuttered room, behind closed drapes, while gunners walked their posts outside and guard dogs prowled the walled perimeter of Bob Pattricia's fortress home. Giamba ached to have an army on the streets, to lead them against the enemy and drive them back beyond the borders of the territory that had been his family's now for over fifty years.

Except that Artie didn't have an army anymore. His meager troops were mostly Bob Pattricia's boys, and while there could not be a question of the underboss's loyalty, it still did not feel right, this leaning on a younger man instead of fighting for himself.

As always, when he thought of Bobby, Art Giamba thought of Jules, and that brought back the shock, the pain of loss he had experienced on learning of his old friend's violent death. Scarpato owed him one for that, and for the raid on his house that morning.

He reached for the chianti bottle, noticed that his hand was trembling again and cursed beneath his breath. No use in trying to dismiss it as a sign of age. He was afraid, and that was weakness of another sort. A weakness of the soul that got inside a man and ate him from the inside out.

Giamba filled his wineglass, drained it, filled it to the brim again. The liquor lit a fire inside him, briefly drove away the doubts that had been plaguing him. About himself. About his family. About his own mortality.

He would be dead right now if it was not for Bolan. The aging mafioso had to laugh aloud at that, amused by the ironic turn of his misfortunes. Everywhere the brotherhood was reeling from this warrior's blows. Its soldiers hunted him, intent on ending his vendetta. But here he was, and he had saved Giamba from disaster a second time. Artie felt that somehow there was something out of kilter. Bolan should have killed him when they met that first time, or again last night...but he had blown away Giamba's enemies instead. Secure now for the moment with the wine at work inside him, Artie wondered if it might have been an omen, pointing on to better days ahead.

Suppose he could recruit this Bolan somehow and use him to eliminate Scarpato. Artie knew that others had tried to take out the soldier before, but no one in the brotherhood had ever come this close. Giamba could not say why Bolan had assisted him, and he didn't even care. There seemed to be an opening for something bigger, and the mafioso did not plan to throw his only chance away.

If he could get in touch with Bolan...

And suppose he couldn't? What if Bolan never called him back? Suppose the goddamned guy left town, or got himself picked off when he went up against Scarpato on his own?

There had been a time when Art Giamba would have bought a ringside seat for Bolan's execution, but times and circumstances changed. He needed Bolan now. He was Giamba's last hope of winning back the territory he had lost throughout the years.

No other family would trespass on his turf once it was known he had the Executioner in tow. Forget about New York, Chicago, all the rest. St. Louis would be riding high with Artie's one-man army standing by to deal with anyone who crossed him.

But he was dreaming now, the mafioso knew. He did not even have the soldier's number, let alone his loyalty, and it would take some damn sweet terms to win Bolan over from his own crusade. Giamba understood vendettas, knew how vengeance motivated men to kill and kill again...and yet, the soldier did not seem to fit that mold.

Whatever motivated Bolan, everybody had a price. If no one had succeeded with the soldier yet, it only meant they had not raised the ante high enough. Giamba had the ingenuity, the will, to do it right. Provided that he had the time.

And time was running short, he realized. Scarpato was not Artie's only enemy these days. He faced another every time he faced a mirror. Around the eyes, the mouth, across his forehead, wrinkles formed a road map to the grave.

Giamba needed time...to put it all together for one last victory. One last triumphant laugh before he passed it all to Bob Pattricia.

But Artie wasn't ready to release his hold upon the empire he had built from nothing. Not just yet.

A gentle rapping on the study door, and Bobby's houseman, Bruno, stuck his head inside.

"You got a phone call, Mr. G.," he said. "You wanna take it here?"

Giamba nodded, waved him in.

"Tha's fine."

The wine was interfering with his speech, but Artie cleared his throat and watched as Bruno entered, carrying a telephone. He bent down toward the baseboard and slipped the little plastic plug into a wall jack, straightening to bring the phone across to where Giamba sat.

"Tha's fine," Giamba said again.

The houseman left and Artie hesitated for a moment with his hand on the receiver, frowning. It was odd to get a phone call here. The other members of his family who knew where he was staying would normally have asked for Bobby. Sure. Except that these were anything but normal times.

He lifted the receiver to his ear, relieved to find that the chianti had removed the trembling from his hands.

"H'lo?"

"Good morning, Artie."

He was sober all at once, his fingers clutching the receiver with such force that he was sure the plastic would shatter. The funereal voice was like a stinging slap across the face.

"Hey, it's you. I wondered when I'd hear from you again."

"You're hearing from me," Bolan answered.

"Sure. Okay. Wha's goin' on?"

"I need more information on Scarpato."

Artie's heart was in his throat. He couldn't answer fast enough. "You name it, an' you got it, guy."

"I'm looking for a place where he might stash a hostage. Someone that he can't afford to be connected with if things turn sour."

Giamba's stomach rumbled at him, and his bladder felt as if it might explode. He clenched his knees, thinking desperately, coming up empty.

"It's gonna take some time," he stalled. "We ain't exac'ly on the best of terms, ya know? I mean, I got my ways of findin' out...but it'll take some time."

"I haven't got much time," the soldier told him flatly. "You don't, either."

He was breaking off, and Giamba knew he had to keep the bastard on the line.

"Hey, wait a sec!" he blurted desperately. "I'll get you what you need, okay? Jus' let me have some slack. You got a number there where I can get in touch with you?"

"*I'll* get in touch with *you*," the Executioner replied. His voice was tinged with Arctic frost.

"Okay, whatever. Say, but listen, while I got you on the line…"

It took a moment for the aging hood to realize that he was talking to himself. The line was dead. He cursed under his breath and slammed the receiver back into its cradle.

Giamba forced himself to sit back in his chair, relax, take stock of what he'd heard. The Executioner was looking for Scarpato, which was easy, and a hostage, which Giamba did not understand at all.

Who could it be?

It wasn't him, and Bob Pattricia was safe inside his house, surrounded by his palace guard. Nobody else was worth the trouble of a snatch. For damn sure, no one else would give Scarpato what he wanted from Giamba. Vince could rub out a dozen hostages and Artie would not bat an eye.

But if the Executioner was interested, then Giamba should be interested, as well. If he could help the soldier with the information that he needed to deliver yet another blow against Scarpato….

The aging mobster realized that he would not need Bolan on the payroll to win this thing. He was after Scarpato, anyway. If the goddamned guy was bent on doing Artie's job free, why should the mobster spoil it for him by suggesting payment?

It was ideal. The Executioner would be doing Giamba's dirty work, and at the same time conserving Artie's meager army, his reserves, his treasury. The thought of final victory was sweet; the thought of total victory free made Artie laugh out loud, a manic cackle that filled the study, echoing around the walls until he sank back in his chair, worn out.

He still had work to do, of course. The hostage was important to Bolan, and if it would hurt Scarpato in some way, Giamba meant to give the soldier every bit of aid he could spare. It would require some calls to find out exactly where Scarpato's hot spots were and where his troops were quartered, but Giamba knew exactly how to do it. Provided that the soldier didn't run ahead of him, and do the job alone before Giamba had an opportunity to win his favor.

Reaching for the telephone again, he heard the warrior's words inside his mind. *"I haven't got much time. You don't, either."*

Giamba did not like the sound of that, but he could not afford to let some cryptic message spook him now. He had a job to do before somebody else could beat him to it.

He had to help Bolan find a nameless, faceless hostage, somewhere in St. Louis.

Simple.

Provided that he had the time.

12

Vince Scarpato watched his soldiers fanning out across the broad expanse of lawn to take their posts around the property. Scarpato shook his head in sheer disgust. The bastards had a sudden urge to do their jobs, but it was too goddamned late.

A gentle breeze was wafting through the paneless full-length window, stirring drapes on either side of him. Stepping through the empty window frame, he felt the shards of shattered glass beneath his feet. They crunched just like the brittle ice that forms on New York sidewalks in the wintertime, reminding him of home.

New York.

Scarpato wished that he was back there now. Or, better still, that he had been back there six damn months ago, and knowing what he knew today. He could have made some changes and saved himself some grief along the way.

The stench of gasoline and oily smoke was in his nostrils now, a grim reminder of the wreckage out in front. It was an hour since the fire department had come and gone, complete with squad cars bringing up the rear.

There had been time to get the bodies out of sight, to pull the damaged gates out front, and then Scarpato had been set upon by every kind of uniform imaginable. Cops and fire marshals, members of the goddamned arson squad, all grinning at him like he was an idiot and making sure he knew they didn't buy a single word he said.

It was humiliating and Vince Scarpato did not take humiliation lightly. Someone was going to pay for all the trouble he had been caused.

The worst of it was that they reached him *here*, inside his sanctuary, where he should have been secure. It shook Scarpato to think that anyone could slip inside his walls, past guards and TV cameras. It was supposed to be the other way around...but then again, his plans all had a tendency to backfire in his face these days.

It had been easy to believe in the beginning. Don Ernesto Marinello confided in him, and Scarpato had read a promise in Don Ernesto's words. There had been a hint of future independence for Scarpato, with a family of his own if he assisted Marinello in securing his birthright.

St. Louis was open territory these days, Marinello had told him. Never mind old Art Giamba and his buddy Jules. They were a joke from coast to coast, these paper capos with their dwindling territory.

It should have been a milk run, in and out, with Artie's head for Marinello on a silver platter, but the old man had shown more fight than they anticipated. Playing hit-and-run, he tied Scarpato up for weeks on end, and in the meantime Marinello lost in New York.

Scarpato shook his head again, amazed that so much rotten luck could squeeze itself into a single person's lifetime. And what was that line about lightning never striking twice? Well, a lightning bolt had taken Ernie Marinello out, you bet. It had blown his ass away, along with something like a dozen other dons from all around the countryside.

Scarpato had been furious and shaken when the headlines gave that lightning bolt a name.

Mack Bolan.

A small, involuntary shudder raced along his spine and lost itself amid the stubble of his close-cropped hair. Still...that was then, and this is now.

There was hope yet of pulling off a coup successfully.

Scarpato scowled, refusing to consider failure as a possibility. If Marinello's eyes had proven bigger than his stomach, that was Ernie's problem, sure, and he had paid for it in spades. But that would not prevent Scarpato from achieving something on his own, provided that he kept his wits about him.

Providing that he didn't get picked off right here, inside his own damned grounds.

Giamba was resisting him tenaciously, and with an energy incredible for someone of his age. Scarpato thought of Bob Pattricia, the hatred Vince had kindled there by ordering the hit on Jules, and wondered if Gambia's youthful underboss was laying strategy these days. It didn't seem to fit, and yet...

Someone had reached him here, inside his home, and if that "Ace"—what did he call himself? Omega, yeah—had moved with more alacrity, Scarpato would be in a body bag by now. It had been slick, perhaps too slick for Bobby or Giamba to conceive and execute alone.

An ugly thought was nagging at him from the shadows of his mind, and Vincent brought it out into the light. Suppose Omega was an Ace. Where did that leave Scarpato in the universal scheme of things?

Ernesto Marinello had informed him early on that he was bringing back the Aces, building them back up to be the awesome fighting force they were in the beginning. The rising capo spent a lot of cash and energy just tracking down survivors of the grim elite, enlisting those who proved receptive, liquidating those who balked or asked for too much thinking time. When he was done, he had controlled a hard-core nucleus of maybe twenty guns, but he had bigger things in mind.

Until Mack Bolan.

And most of Marinello's hard force went down with him on Long Island, except for three who had accompanied Scarpato to St. Louis as the spearhead of his expeditionary force.

The Ace called Stone was second in command, but there were times when Vincent thought he might be getting too damned big for everybody's good. He didn't show Scarpato the respect a capo deserved, and there were times when he had countermanded little orders, asserting his authority and making Vincent wonder if there might be something going on he didn't know about.

It made Vincent wonder what his Ace was up to, whom he might be working for behind the scenes. It made him wonder if Omega was a phony Ace at all, or if he had been sent by someone else to test Scarpato's fortress, feel him out for weaknesses and vantage points.

A muffled sound behind him made the mafioso jump. He spun around to find the Black Ace, Stone, regarding him with blank, impassive eyes from just inside the shattered window.

"What have you got?" Scarpato tried to sound commanding, realized before he got the sentence out how lame it sounded.

"Enough to know our ringer wasn't sent by any of the other families."

"Oh, yeah? How can you be so sure?"

"Technology, for one thing," Stone replied. "You ever know a gunner who would booby-trap his own damned car to use as a diversion?"

Scarpato thought about it, finally shook his head. "Nobody I can think of."

"Right," the Ace agreed. "It takes a special kind of thinking to prepare yourself that way. A special kind of mind." He hesitated, watching Vince Scarpato's face. "I'd say it takes a military mind."

"So what?" Scarpato asked. "You think Giamba's got some kinda supercommando on his payroll?"

The Ace dropped into an easy chair without waiting to be asked. And he was smiling at the would-be capo as he shook his head.

"I told you he didn't come from any of the families. Giamba doesn't have that kind of talent in his ranks."

"Okay. So, what the hell..."

Stone sighed, impatient, like a teacher grappling with a marginally retarded child. "Think about it, Vince. Do you know *anybody* with a military background who might want to see you dead?"

Scarpato thought about it, fuming at the way Stone put himself upon a first-name basis with his nominal superior. He came up empty, and he wished he could have called on Ernie Marinello for some help in sorting out the pieces of the puzzle. But Ernie was dead, of course. He had been killed by—

"Mack Bolan?"

"Bingo."

Stone was grinning at him like a hungry weasel, nodding slowly. Scarpato felt an icy fist begin to squeeze his heart, restricting blood flow to his brain and touching off a buzzing in his ears. A headache throbbed to life behind his eyes, and he reached the chair before his legs gave way.

"Mack Bolan."

Vincent realized that he was staring like a basket case and caught himself, the frown regaining something of its early confidence as he pinned Stone beneath an icy stare.

"What makes you think so?" he demanded.

"Tactics, mostly, like I said. Besides, I've heard that fake Omega handle once before, when he was in the neighborhood."

Scarpato raised an eyebrow, curious. "I never knew you met the guy before."

"We didn't *meet*. I said he was around. We missed each other by an hour or so, when he was tearing through Atlanta some time back."

A lucky break for you, Scarpato thought, and smiled at his enforcer, feeling he had finally found a weakness in the cool, commanding Ace. The guy had slipped past Bolan once, and now he must be feeling something of the same cold fear Scarpato held inside himself. That is, if he was leveling with Vincent now, instead of running down some bullshit line for reasons of his own.

"What if you're wrong? What if it's someone else?"

Stone shook his head. "I know the talent that's available. I know my men. We closed the net around him quick enough this morning, and we would have had him if it wasn't for the fireworks out front. That's Bolan, all the way."

Scarpato frowned, no longer certain of himself. "So what's he want from me?"

"What does he ever want? He's got it in for the brotherhood, and don't forget he helped Giamba once before."

"That goddamn Artie! What the hell's so special that he charms this Bolan, anyway?"

Stone shrugged. "Who knows. Who *cares*? Giamba won't be charming anyone this time tomorrow."

"Yeah? I wouldn't be so sure."

"You need more confidence," the Ace informed him, not without a trace of sarcasm. "Anyway, this new approach will tie the soldier's hands."

"You say."

"That's right, I say. The bastard's never dropped the hammer on a cop, not even when they had him cornered. Hell, he's queer that way, I guess. Once Newman sends his uniforms against Giamba and Pattricia, it's over."

"Supposin' Bolan doesn't know that?" Vince challenged, glaring at his chief enforcer.

"Then we take him out," the Ace replied, as if it was the least of his concerns.

"You had one crack at that already."

"We were unprepared."

"Goddammit, I'm not paying for your men to sit around here on their asses unprepared!"

"I meant that we were unprepared for Bolan," Stone amended, looking somewhat shaken for the first time in the conversation. "It takes a special kind of preparation for that guy."

"You think you've got it in you?"

Stone was giving off defensive vibes, and Vince Scarpato was elated by the tiny victory but kept the feelings to himself.

"He's as good as in the bag," the Ace replied, but there was something of a hesitance about his tone.

"Okay." Scarpato spoke with a confidence he didn't feel. "I leave it in your hands. But if you let me down..."

He did not have to spell it out. The Ace was not exactly shaking, no, but now he knew his life was riding on the line along with Scarpato's and the rest.

"It's done," Stone said as he excused himself. The study door clicked shut behind him, and Scarpato was alone.

Mack Bolan in St. Louis.

Dammit!

If Stone was right, there was a chance the soldier might be going for a clean sweep of the Marinello family remnants, making sure there were no loose ends left to haunt him later. And then again, the bastard might be working for Giamba, though Scarpato would not hope to puzzle out the hows and whys of that arrangement if he took a thousand years.

But what if Stone was wrong?

Worse yet, what if he was deliberately lying through his teeth, deceiving his superiors for some ulterior reasons of his own?

If he was wrong, or lying, then Bolan wasn't in St. Louis, after all. And that would mean that someone else had conned his way through Vince's troops and right into his goddamned house.

Who had that kind of nerve, aside from Bolan? Who possessed the skill and guts to risk it all on an explosive grandstand play such as Scarpato had been witness to that morning?

Vincent knew the answer, and it chilled him to the bone.

An Ace would have the guts, the knowledge. Sure.

A real Black Ace.

Like Stone.

And if Omega *was* legitimate, then what of Stone's "exposure," his revelations on the phony calling card? Was Stone the victim of a lethal prank himself, or was he setting up Scarpato for a long, hard fall?

The questions jostled for position in the mafioso's throbbing skull until he finally forced them back into the shadows, concentrating on the task at hand.

He had a war to win, and he had already put the wheels in motion for a bold end run that would deprive Mack Bolan—or Omega, or whoever—of his edge in siding with Giamba. With the law on Vince's side, applying heat to Artie's family all over town, there would be no way Vince could lose.

Unless, of course, some stranger waltzed into his house and blew his brains out.

A shiver raced along Scarpato's spine, and he was scowling, more from anger than from fear. It didn't matter to him now if Bolan was the opposition. Let him come. Scarpato had some scores to settle—for himself, for Ernie Marinello, for the whole damned brotherhood.

And if it should turn out that Stone was working on an angle of his own, deceiving his superiors, Scarpato would have time enough to deal with him when he had finished mopping up Giamba and Pattricia, securing St. Louis for himself.

He would have all the time in the world to deal with traitors and false friends.

Before he finished with them all, they would be pleading for the sweet release of death, and maybe he would let them find it. In his own time. In his own way. When he was satisfied that they had been repaid for all their treachery.

The bloody vision brought a beatific smile to Vince Scarpato's face. The chill was gone, and he was in control again. As it was meant to be.

He would be looking forward to the next encounter with his enemies. They would be in for some surprises, including Stone, and now the mafioso felt a rising sense of expectation, almost an elation, he had not experienced in years. Not since he killed a human being for the first time.

13

The numbers bank was situated one flight up, above a pool hall on the fringe of the St. Louis ghetto. Like the bars and pawnshops that surrounded it, the pool hall had a black proprietor but was, in fact, the property of a Caucasian landlord. With the exception of the owner's front man and his muscle, members of a local street gang called the Mutilators, no one in the seamy neighborhood had ever learned the landlord's name.

But Bolan knew it.

The landlord's name was Vince Scarpato.

He had moved in among the street gangs early, alternating punishments with payoffs as he sought to undermine Giamba's source of income from the numbers racket. And he had succeeded, to a point. His beachhead was substantial, but the cut demanded by New York was larger than Giamba ever claimed, and many of the locals were resisting, siding with Giamba and Pattricia in a business on the brink of civil war.

The war had been a long time coming, thanks to Art Giamba's tolerance, his fear of biting off a bigger piece than he could chew, and now the neighborhood was ready to explode.

And Bolan had come to light the fuse.

A single drive-by told him all he had to know. He marked the flashy Lincoln pimp mobile out front, a pair of Mutilators lounging in the alley to the rear, protecting their employer's flank. They could be trouble if they stopped him on the street, before he had a chance to get in range, and he decided it would have to be the front door.

He circled once around the block and parked beyond the Continental, in a corner slot that guaranteed he would not find himself wedged in if it was necessary to depart at speed. A short walk back, and Bolan felt the hostile curiosity of passersby, examining his whiteness with suspicion and mistrust before he ducked inside the poolroom.

An ancient ceiling fan was struggling to move the musty air around inside the place, and it was failing miserably. The billiard parlor stank of perspiration, urine and accumulated smoke from cheap cigars. Bolan shied away from contact with the scattered furniture as he allowed his eyes to grow accustomed to the murk.

Behind an imitation hardwood bar, a white-haired man was polishing what had to be the only clean glass in the place, deliberately avoiding any glance in the direction of the door. A single Mutilator, long and lean, was perched upon a bar stool, eyeing Bolan with contempt and sucking on a Coors.

The Executioner moved past a standing rack of cues, toward the stairs in back. He heard the Mutilator slide off his stool and hesitated in midstride, expecting an attack, but when he looked around the lanky youth was disappearing through the double doors.

He would be back, no doubt, with reinforcements to assist him if the boss should need some help, but for the moment Bolan put him out of mind. His business lay upstairs, and there was ample danger there to occupy the soldier's mind.

The stairs were covered with a leprous carpeting that muffled Bolan's footsteps. The stairwell was in darkness save for pasty daylight pooled around its base and the anemic glow of one tired light bulb on the upstairs landing. Bolan had the sleek Beretta in his hand before he started climbing, safety off, and halfway up he knew that he would need it.

A sentry was on station at the entrance to the numbers bank. Kicked back against the wall in what appeared to be a metal folding chair, the guy was half asleep and fading fast. From all appearances, he was about to drop the sawed-off scattergun that lay across his lap.

And Bolan could have taken him that way except for purest chance. Another stride, and the thirteenth riser groaned beneath his weight, became a muffled squeal...once more the warrior knew that nothing ever came the easy way.

The sentry jerked erect, his shotgun rising, tracking onto target now before his mind could struggle back to consciousness. A sleepy finger missed the trigger guard, came back to try again—

And Bolan never let him have that second chance.

The 93-R whispered, once, a silenced parabellum round closing the gap between them, opening another in the sentry's forehead and propelling him against the wall. His folding chair collapsed and pinned him there, propped back against the wall, his knees against his chin, the stubby shotgun barrel poking between his knees like some outrageous phallic symbol.

Bolan rushed the door and one explosive kick beside the lock drove it against the inside wall. He entered, the Beretta probing ahead of him, its muzzle swinging back and forth to cover everybody in the room.

Four men, three of them black, were sitting around a desk. The fourth was a Mafia gorilla complete with pinstriped suit. One hand was already tucked inside his jacket, reaching for the iron he carried there. On either side of him the lanky dudes in flashy suits were scrambling for daylight, digging for hardware, intent upon the exit Bolan occupied.

He took the mafioso first, a parabellum double punch drilling him and driving him backward, out of frame and out of mind.

On Bolan's left, the number two had reached his weapon, had it in his hand...but he would never have the chance to fire. A silenced mangler punched between his snarling teeth and lifted him completely off his feet, propelling him against a filing cabinet, then he began to slide away, responding to the call of gravity.

And number three had time enough to squeeze the trigger once, his bullet high and wide, deflected by the filing cabinets, drilling through a flimsy plaster wall. The Executioner replied with smooth precision, stroking off a single round that stretched his target out across the desk, his leaking head directly in the startled banker's lap.

Bolan stook before the desk, his autoloader leveled at the bulging eyes, its muzzle picking out a point between them. But the guy was rigid in his chair, with both hands showing, his fish-lips working soundlessly for several heartbeats until he finally found his voice.

"Hey, man...there must be some mistake."

"You made it," Bolan told him simply, watching nervous perspiration bead along his brow.

"Well...say...le's talk, awright?"

"Let's not. I've got a message for Scarpato, and I'm leaving it with you, unless you think it's more than you can handle."

Sudden hope behind the eyes—and instant recognition of the grim alternative for failure, for resistance.

"Hey, we're jus' like that." One hand came off the desk top, two fingers crossed, and then the guy thought better of it, eased the hand back down, fingers splayed to let the soldier see he had no weapon. "Tell me what you need—I pass it on."

"Scarpato's got a package that belongs to me," Bolan said. "I want it back. If it's been damaged, he can kiss it all goodbye."

The banker soaked it in, already nodding, dredging up a feeble smile. He was anxious to please, to survive.

"I got it, man. I'll pass it on."

"You do that, man."

A sudden thought traced worry lines between the banker's eyes. "Supposin' he should ask who lef' the word? I mean...we ain't been introduced, you know?"

When Bolan reached across the desk, the banker flinched instinctively, recoiling from the touch of Sudden Death. His progress was arrested by the wall, two feet behind him, and he sat there, staring, as the soldier placed a small, metallic object in the middle of the faceless gunner's chest, above the silent heart.

A marksman's medal.

"I'll be in touch again if Vinnie doesn't get the word."

The banker's voice was trapped between a whisper and a wheeze. "He'll get it, man. It's on the way."

The soldier moved away from there, relieved to find that none of the expected Mutilator reinforcements had arrived downstairs. He had no wish to spark a bloodbath here. He had achieved his purpose with the banker, and he still had other stops to make before he risked a major confrontation with Scarpato's men.

He had begun to spread the word, and he was far from finished.

Before the afternoon was out, Scarpato would be sick of hearing from him.

Sick to death.

JOEY SPINOZA HAD A GREAT RESPECT for science. Never mind that he had been a sixth-grade dropout in the Bronx, with numerous suspensions on his record for assault, theft and vandalism in the public schools. You live and learn, and Joey, in adulthood, had his reasons for appreciating all that modern science had achieved.

It was a miracle that half a dozen eggheads in their starchy whites could take a dash of this, a pinch of that and turn out so much PCP in record time. He marveled at the way they worked together, understanding everything the printed labels had to say, avoiding the mistakes that would have blown them all to hell and back again.

He knew that PCP was actually a tranquilizer used on animals...and that was just another mystery to puzzle over on those long rides to the bank. Whatever its effect on cows and horses, it had never tranquilized a human being in Spinoza's own experience. It *energized* them, sure, and gave them strength like Superman or Wonder Woman in the comics Joey liked to ''read,'' avoiding words and concentrating on the pictures, where the action lay. Another miracle. You bet.

Of course, the profits made on PCP could not compare with those on good cocaine, but Joey and his eggheads handled both, supplying high-school punks and members of the Gucci crowd with equanimity, accepting pocket change and crumpled dollar bills or crisp new C-notes, either way it came.

Another month or two of rising profits, and Scarpato would begin to realize how much Spinoza had been doing for him since they hit St. Louis and began attacking Art Giamba's pocketbook. Another month or two, yes, and Joey would be ready to request a place beside Scarpato in the family he was forming to run the city. With Vince Scarpato, there would be room for swift advancement through the ranks.

Providing that Spinoza played his cards right.

Spinoza watched the lab technicians in their whites, intent upon their business, the bunsen burner flames reflected in their horn-rims, giving them that wild mad-doctor look that made him shake his head and chuckle through his surgical mask. He didn't have a damned idea of how they did it, but he didn't care, as long as they kept grinding out the magic powders for his salesmen on the streets.

One of the chemists straightened, his head cocked toward the blacked-out windows, listening, straining to hear a sound that had escaped Spinoza altogether. The enforcer craned forward on his stool, watching the chemist and listening...

To nothing.

The guy shrugged, looking foolish in his mask and horn-rims, the loose-fitting lab smock. He went back to his job, and Spinoza began to relax, silently cursing the inbred paranoia of the academics he was forced to baby-sit around the lab.

They wouldn't know a danger situation if it slithered up one leg and bit them on the ass, he thought. Unless their problem came out of a test tube, they were helpless, children afraid of the dark.

And Spinoza had to admit that he liked it that way.

The paranoia kept them sharp, and the attendant insecurity kept all of them in line. The lab men were afraid of him as much as of arrest, and rightly so. If one of them should try to rat, go into business for himself or someone else...

Spinoza thought he was hallucinating when the blacked-out window imploded into razor shrapnel, peppering the lab. The gunner vaulted off his stool, already digging for the Magnum underneath his jacket as a tall intruder came out of a shoulder roll behind the tables, suddenly erect and shooting from the hip.

The guy was dressed in military camouflage from head to heels, and he was handling his Uzi submachine gun like a pro. One burst demolishing several hundred dollars' worth of glassware on the trestle tables, kicking up a priceless cloud of flake and PCP that had the lab men gagging, running back and forth. A second blast caught two of the technicians on the run and rolled them up, their whites all flecked with scarlet now.

Spinoza had his Magnum out, tracking onto target when the soldier spotted him and hit a crouch, the Uzi sliding out to meet his challenge. He saw the wrinkling muzzle flash, and then his legs were cut from under him, the short, staccato sounds arriving on the heels of monumental pain as Joey felt his kneecaps go, the floor rush up to meet his face.

You never hear the shot that kills you, but he had heard those shots all right, and he was still alive. So far.

A pair of military boots monopolized his field of vision, one detaching from the other long enough to catch his Magnum with a toe and send it skittering across the floor. Spinoza tried to roll away, but pain had sapped his strength, and he was helpless when the soldier reached down for him, catching him beneath the arms and lifting him.

The guy half dragged, half carried Joey through the dusty litter of the lab, his limp extremities describing bloody patterns in the crystal snowdrifts. At the windowsill, his captor stepped outside, then reached back to hoist Spinoza clear, not speaking, scarcely breathing hard as he proceeded with his human bundle up the fire escape and to the roof.

He left Spinoza propped against the safety railing, and he disappeared again, descending on the rusty fire escape. The metal structure made a rasping sound of protest, but it held.

And Joey knew, too late, exactly what the chemist had been listening for before the roof fell in.

The goddamned fire escape.

Beneath him, Joey felt the shudder of a small explosion, heard it seconds later through the shattered windows of the lab. And he was smelling acrid smoke before the soldier reappeared, the painted hands and face all sooty now, the graveyard eyes intent upon Spinoza as he crouched at the mafioso's side.

"You're out of business," he explained unnecessarily.

"Okay."

It took Spinoza's strength to get it out, and there was nothing more to say.

"Scarpato has a package that belongs to me," the soldier said. "I want it back intact. The heat stays on until he comes across."

Spinoza nodded slowly, understanding why he had been spared. He was to be the gunner's errand boy, although he wouldn't get much mileage out of these legs now.

A fire alarm was jangling in the alleyway below. The soldier straightened and fished a hand inside one of his many pockets, coming out with a metallic object, which he dropped into Spinoza's lap.

A marksman's medal.

But what the hell...?

Spinoza's mind was trying to make sense of that, and when it hit him like a blow above the heart he glanced up fearfully.

And found himself alone.

The big commando was gone.

Spinoza settled back and tried to concentrate on anything besides the pain. At last, he settled on the message he would give Scarpato, if he lived. If help arrived before the ancient building burned right out from under him and fried him like a burger on a barbecue.

He had a message for the capo, and he did not dare forget a single word of it. His life was riding on delivery, and Joey did not plan to throw it all away. In fact, he would enjoy the look on Vince's face when he received the word.

Scarpato owed him that much, anyway. For all his trouble. For his legs. And for the empire Joey knew he would never share.

The would-be capo owed him, and he was going to pay. In full.

BOLAN HELD THE UZI'S TRIGGER down and let the stubby weapon empty in one protracted burst, the parabellum manglers raking corrugated metal walls and stacks of packing crates. A sluggish gunner went down kicking, thrashed across the bloody concrete for a moment, finally lay still.

And Bolan was slamming home a fresh magazine, already moving out for other cover when the hostile weapons opened up again, their chorus sounding like a clap of thunder in the echo chamber of the warehouse. The soldier hit a flying shoulder roll, came up behind an unattended fork lift, bullets ringing off the metalwork above him, chipping at the cement floor on either side.

Scarpato's warehouse on the riverfront had suddenly become a trap, and Bolan knew that he could lose it here within the next few moments if he let his guard down for an instant. He was cornered and outnumbered, but it wasn't over yet.

He had anticipated light security around Scarpato's warehouse during daylight hours, with a rental cop or two on hand to watch for vandals. Instead, he had unknowingly intruded on a group of hungry gunners marking time between engagements with Giamba's troops, and one of them had spotted him before he had a chance to disengage. He had already taken three of them, but that left eight or nine alive and waiting for a chance to bring him down.

The warehouse was a temporary storage place for contraband of every sort, from stolen cigarettes, appliances and guns to bootleg liquor, records, videocassettes. The illicit goods arrived by truck, by train, by river barge and quickly vanished into retail outlets scattered all around St. Louis, making money for Scarpato while it chipped away at Art Giamba's income.

The warrior's plan had been to torch Scarpato's warehouse, leave message with the watchman if he found one and be on to other targets. Instead, the Executioner was fighting for his life, and time was running out as the hostile gunners moved to close the ring about him.

Bolan did not plan to make it easy for them. Squeezing off a measured bust to keep them back and down, he ducked beneath a blizzard of return fire, freed the round white phosphorous grenade from his munitions harness, pulled the pin. The can's five-second fuse would not allow his adversaries time to pitch it back, and he was counting on their anger and surprise to further slow reaction time, provide him with the edge required to make his desperate gamble work.

The soldier came erect behind the forklift, squeezing off another automatic burst, his Uzi sweeping back and forth. His enemies were scrambling for cover when he made the pitch, and Bolan watched the thermite egg bounce once atop a pile of crates before it disappeared from sight.

Retreating in the face of scattered pistol fire, he crouched behind the forklift, waiting, running down the doomsday numbers in his mind. Another second now, and then the phosphorous grenade exploded with a whooosh of super-heated air, expelling smoke and white-hot streamers that would eat through corrugated steel and packing crates and human flesh with equal ease, igniting scores of secondary fires wherever hissing coals touched down.

He heard a gunner screaming near the center of the spreading conflagration, risked a glance in time to see the leaping human torch clear cover, running blindly now. His comrades were abandoning the ship, and Bolan waited for them to reveal themselves, the Uzi awaiting targets.

A rush of movement on his left, and two men cleared the shadow of a boxed refrigerator, running for their lives without a backward glance. They made it halfway to the double doors before a stream of parabellum manglers overtook them and brought them down. They sprawled together on the concrete, mingling their blood.

Another pistolero, breaking to the right, and Bolan stroked the Uzi's trigger lightly for a 3-round burst that took his face off.

The hostile fire was spotty now, and careless. They were firing for the hell of it, the soldier knew, defying fear of death by making noise and knowing all the while that they would have to break for it or burn.

They broke for it, all four at once, and Bolan heard them coming now, despite the hungry crackling of the flames. He had the Uzi leveled, waiting, and he held the trigger down as they emerged from cover, ripping through the stubby weapon's load at 750 rounds per minute. Bolan stitched a blazing figure-eight around the four and watched them scatter, stagger, reel and fall. One of them struggled briefly, tried to rise, then melted into death among the others, leaking life and hope through mortal wounds.

Bolan dropped a marksman's medal on the forklift's seat and took himself away from there. The fire was growing, feeding on itself and on Scarpato's contraband, already sending smoky feelers out to prod the fallen bodies where they lay. Outside, he found a fire alarm and smashed it with the Uzi's metal folding stock, proceeding in the direction of his rental car and safety.

The direction of another target, right.

Scarpato would receive his message, loud and clear, despite the lack of living messengers to bear the word. Another dozen soldiers lost, his warehouse going up in smoke...The would-be capo from New York would soon be totting up his losses, sure. He would be anxious to respond, in one way or another, to the Bolan blitz.

Scarpato might release the girl unharmed and hope for one of Bolan's rare but celebrated truces.

Or he might react the other way, coming out swinging hard with everything he had.

The hellfire warrior knew his odds. He understood his enemy.

And Bolan would be waiting for Scarpato, whichever way he came.

14

Captain Tom Postum watched the firemen stripping off their respirator masks and shedding heavy tanks of oxygen, already reeling in their hoses, making ready to leave the warehouse. The arson team would linger on awhile but it was over for the front-line troops.

A stench of burning cloaked the waterfront and mingled with the old, familiar river smells, but nothing could dilute the subtle, sickly sweetness of that dark odor. And it made Postum glad that he had passed on lunch.

He scanned the line of shrouded corpses stretched out in the shadow of the warehouse, wrinkling his nose because the stench was rising off them as much as from the warehouse. And the captain knew it would take dental records to identify them...if they were ever identified at all.

"Some friggin' mess." The short lieutenant at his side spoke softly, almost reverently in the presence of the dead.

Tom Postum nodded. "Yeah. Some mess."

"You figure Artie caught 'em by surprise?"

"I wouldn't want to second-guess the lab on this one."

Postum drifted toward the warehouse, skirting the sheeted bodies, the lieutenant on his heels. The double sliding doors were standing open now, although they had been warped by heat and would no longer open all the way. The strike-force captain hesitated for a moment prior to entering, examining the corrugated metal doors.

"See that?"

He pointed out two holes the size of silver dollars, set perhaps a yard apart, their blackened edges still hot enough to sear the fingertips.

"White phosphorous?"

"I'd say."

"I haven't seen that since Da Nang." The short lieutenant frowned. "Giamba and Pattricia are playing rough."

Postum kept his opinion to himself and moved inside. The concrete floors were flooded, and he had to watch his step. Despite the open doors, it was smoky in the warehouse, and the stench of burning flesh was stronger here. The captain knew at once that he had stepped into a charnel house.

The lieutenant whistled softly, scanning row on row of blackened crates, some of them broken open and water stained.

"Scarpato had a lot of shit in here." He sniffed the smoky air. "I'd say we found ourselves that load of hijacked cigarettes."

"You'll never tie New York to any of this mess."

"Too bad."

"Too bad is right."

"Well, if it's any consolation, Tom, the bastard lost a lot more here than any court would fine him on a first offense."

The strike-force captain frowned. It wasn't any kind of consolation at all.

He recognized the leader of the arson team and flagged him down. A couple of detectives from his strike force were already huddled with the fire department's team, comparing their preliminary notes, but Postum knew what they would find.

His friend from arson spelled it out.

"The fire was definitely of incendiary origin, in case you couldn't guess. Some kind of chemical explosive was employed to set it off. I'll need a lab report to pin it down for sure, but from the visuals, I'd say that it was thermite. Probably a military-style grenade.

"Okay. So, what about the casualties?"

The man from arson made a sour face and shook his head. "They're dead. They burned."

"All right. I'll need an inventory of the stock on hand—what's left of it."

"No sweat."

A homicide detective had been examining apparent bullet scars on the blackened carcass of a forklift parked against the northern wall, and now his voice was excited as he hailed Tom Postum. "Say, Captain, over here!"

"What have you got?"

With stainless forceps the detective lifted something small, metallic, from among the sagging springs that had comprised the forklift's seat. Their leather covering and cotton padding had been burned away, reduced to ash, but something had remained. It glittered dully as the homicide investigator dropped it in a plastic bag and tagged it with his own initials, handed it across to Postum for examination.

Cautiously the strike-force captain turned the bag over in his hands, pretending for a moment that he did not recognize the marksman's medal.

"What the hell?"

"Some kind of military decoration."

Postum told them what it was, returned it to the young detective, watching as he took it gingerly, as if afraid that it might bite.

"Well, I'll be damned."

The lieutenant shook his head disgustedly, a frown etched deep into his meaty face. "I heard the guy was still alive, but shit..."

"What guy?" the young detective asked. "You know who did all this?"

"I've got a fair idea," Postum said.

"You ever hear the name Mack Bolan?" his lieutenant asked rhetorically.

"Well, sure." It took another heartbeat for the message to soak in. "You mean...right here?"

"It's possible," Postum said. "We can't confirm it yet."

"I'd say it's pretty well confirmed."

The captain turned on the lieutenant, pinning him with frosty eyes. "It's damn well *not* confirmed. You know as well as I do you can buy those medals at a hundred different shops and swap meets here in town."

"You saying it's a smoke screen, Captain?"

"What I'm saying is we check it out from every angle, and refrain from jumping to conclusions. If Giamba's setting up a blind, I want to know about it."

But the words had left an unpleasant taste behind. And Postum knew that this was no red herring, no elaborate blind to keep detectives chasing shadows while Giamba and Pattricia settled things with Vince Scarpato on their own. The strike-force captain wished it was that simple.

And in a way it was.

Tom Postum wondered why he felt compelled to cover for the Executioner. The strike-force captain knew precisely who had trashed Scarpato's warehouse and the hoods inside it, just as he had known who was behind the other shootings at odd strategic points around the city.

Bolan was attacking, and carrying his private brand of warfare to the enemy. The stakes were high, and Bolan might not be successful...but at least the guy was doing something.

Still, Postum wondered at his own reaction to the lieutenant's logical assumption. Did he owe Mack Bolan something? Was he in the big man's debt?

The answer was an easy one. Of course. He owed his life to Bolan, and there was nothing he could ever do to pay that debt in full.

But that was private, and it had no relation to his duty to the badge he wore.

Like hell.

With twenty years in harness, Postum knew it was impossible to separate the two—the private and the public life—to any great degree. A man might have his secret sins, but every time he buckled on a gun he brought his private thoughts and attitudes along. There were no perfect cops, no magically detached machines in human form who left their hearts and minds behind them when they donned the uniform.

Tom Postum was a cop, and good at what he did...but first of all, he was a *man*. That made him fallible, imperfect, and eminently human underneath his shield.

He had originally joined the force for reasons that were strictly personal. A firm belief in justice under law, for instance. A desire to see that goodness triumphed over evil in the end. Except there wasn't any end, as far as he could see. Instead of victory, there were a thousand stalemates where the adversaries faced each other briefly, backed away, and tried again from other angles.

It had become a game and Postum couldn't quite get used to that. Not even after twenty years.

He still believed in law and justice, though the two were sometimes mutually exclusive now. And he believed in working problems out within "the system," even though the slick machinery was rusty now, and prone to jamming at the worst of times.

Recently Postum had begun to wonder if the system really worked at all.

He thought a lot about the victims, lately, and the way that they had been forgotten in a system set up to protect them from the cannibals. He sat in court and watched indictments thrown away on technicalities, dismissed upon the flimsiest of motions, in a process that was little more than a revolving door for putting felons on the streets. The victims paid—in blood and tears, in broken dreams and shattered lives—but where was justice in the scheme of things?

One man, at least, had found its pulse, and he was doing something to redeem the broken promises. One man had taken all the weight upon himself, and he was drowning, but he was taking plenty of the heavies with him for damn sure.

If there was a way to help him out, extend a hand of friendship...

No.

The Executioner was everything that Postum had despised when he emerged from the police academy and started working on the streets. The guy was a vigilante and a killer, no doubt about it. A self-appointed law unto himself. Each time he pulled the trigger, he was targeting the Constitution, attacking everything Tom Postum stood for.

Except that the soldier had never dropped the hammer on a cop, or on an innocent civilian. And that had to count for something. If Bolan chose his targets independently, at least he chose them well. And unlike other vigilantes out of history, the modern "Death Squads" and their ilk, he had no private ax to grind, no secret prejudice or profit motive to distort his aim.

The guy was fighting on behalf of justice, and that made Postum's job a thousand times more difficult.

For he would have to bring the soldier down.

It was his duty—to the badge he wore, the oath that he had taken when he put it on. If he allowed a private Executioner to stay at large, preempting the established courts, he would be throwing in the towel, surrendering his own beliefs in justice and the rule of law.

It sounded hollow, and the strike-force captain was concerned by what was happening inside him now. The Executioner had saved his life, but that did not relieve Postum of his duty to the law, the citizens who paid his salary each week. He owed them safety from open warfare in the streets, from trigger-happy vermin who mistook the city for a giant free-fire zone.

And yet a part of him would gladly have retreated, left the field to Bolan and his own dramatic brand of war, content to sweep up his leavings and go from there. Assuming that the system was corrupt or simply inefficient, why not tear it down and try again? Why bother going through the motions when they got you nowhere? It was so much easier to strike a match and watch the mother burn.

Except that Postum was too civilized for that.

And so was Bolan.

The warrior wasn't fighting to destroy, but rather to preserve a way of life, a system that was better, even in decay, than any of the grim alternatives. The goddamned guy had made himself a living sacrifice, surrendering his future in a bid to make the system run the way it was supposed to. And he was a single-handed wrecking crew, intent on trashing anyone who tried to soil the dream.

Tom Postum wished that he could help...and knew that he could only try to bring the soldier down. No matter what had passed between them in another place and time, the captain saw his duty now, and he would act on it when the opportunity arose.

It was a goddamned shame.

The smoky atmosphere inside was working on his eyes, his sinuses, and Postum stepped outside to clear his head. The short lieutenant stayed behind to huddle with the man from homicide, and Postum could imagine what the two of them would have to say about him when his back was turned.

No matter.

It was simply caution, a demand for certainty, which made him question Bolan's presence here. It would not be enough to know the guy was guilty, if they could not prove it in a court of law.

But Postum knew that it would never get that far. No way. They hadn't built the jail that could contain Mack Bolan, or protect him from the army of assassins who would stalk him inside the walls.

Mack Bolan was a dead man, and had been from the day he took up arms against the Mafia.

But at the same time he was more alive than any other man Postum knew.

The strike-force captain would have given almost anything for just a fraction of the Executioner's vitality, his strength of will and purpose as he fought alone, against the odds. Instead, it was Tom Postum's job to throttle that vitality, to make damned sure no spark remained behind to kindle other fires.

The sour taste was back in Postum's mouth, the burning in his eyes, and smoke had nothing in the world to do with it. Hell, no. The veteran cop was sickened by the thought of facing Bolan, killing him.

Because he knew the guy would not surrender...any more than he would violently resist arrest. If it came to that, he would complete the sacrifice that had begun so long ago and far away. It would be Postum's task to wield the sacrificial knife.

And it would be his curse to live with that through every waking moment of his life.

15

Vince Scarpato had been trying desperately to hit Giamba and his allies where it hurt the most—directly in the wallet—and the Executioner derived a certain pleasure now from paying back the New York thug in kind.

Already he had cost Scarpato thousands on the warehouse and the powder factory alone. The damaged limousines were running up a separate tab, and never mind the cost of trying to replace the soldiers he had killed. For Vince Scarpato in St. Louis, there were simply no replacements to be had.

New York's estranged ambassador was hurting, sure, but not enough to satisfy the Executioner. He would not rest until Scarpato had been crushed, humiliated. Not until he had surrendered Bonnie Newman. The warrior would be satisfied after he had stripped Scarpato of his hostage, of his budding empire and his life.

But not just yet.

Bolan needed cash, for working capital and to support the secret strongbase manned by brother Johnny back in Southern California. It was poetic justice that his enemies should finance Bolan's war, and hence their own destruction, with the funds that they had stolen from so many innocents throughout the years.

His target was a combination betting room and booking "office" that Scarpato ran downtown, concealed behind a well-appointed bar and grill. The "bank" was going strong, by all accounts, and it was overdue for an encounter with the Executioner.

He circled twice around the block and satisfied himself that the pedestrians he spotted on the street were only that, and nothing more. A parking space downrange had opened between his first and second pass; he slid the rental into it and killed the engine, double-checking the Beretta's load, his extra magazines, before he locked it up and ambled back in the direction of the bar.

Inside the place was dark and cool—a drinker's bar, where food would be a mere distraction from the main event. It took a moment for his pupils to adapt, and then he struck off toward the rear in the direction of a door marked Private. Bolan scanned the clutch of half a dozen customers against the bar, ignored the barkeep with his quizzical expression, concentrating on a solitary hard-eyed type who manned a table near the private office door.

The sentry had him spotted, and the guy was pushing back his chair now, rising to his full, impressive six foot six. His jacket was unbuttoned, providing easy access to the shoulder holster underneath. As Bolan closed in, the watchdog took a sidestep, interposed himself between the new arrival and the office door.

"The crapper's over there," he growled, an index finger jabbing off to Bolan's right, to indicate an archway open on a lighted corridor behind the bar.

"No thanks. I'm looking for the banker," Bolan said.

"I guess you got your wires crossed, dude. You can't make no deposits in a bar."

The Executioner put Arctic edges on his tone. "I haven't got the time to dick around while you go through a stand-up comedy routine," he snarled. "I've got a message for the banker and it's urgent, straight from Mr. Stone."

It was a risk without his ace in hand to back it up, but Bolan saw a flicker behind the gunner's eyes. Stone's name had power here, perhaps enough to see the warrior through and out the other side alive.

"I'll have to check," the sentry told him grudgingly.

"You do that, guy." The soldier made a show of glancing at his watch. "And when the Feds show up to bust this dump, I'll tell 'em that you're busy jerking off."

He had the goon's attention now.

"What Feds? Nobody told me anything about no raid."

Bolan feigned surprise, commingled with disgust. "Well, shit. We're damn near out of time already. Are you gonna let me in there now, or do you wanna tell Scarpato that you let a raiding party take his main back office by surprise?"

The gunner spent another heartbeat chewing on it, then he stepped aside and used his pass key to admit the Executioner. Still unconvinced, he stuck with Bolan, tailing him inside the combination betting room and counting house.

One wall consisted of a giant tote board bearing names of horses and athletic teams, together with the odds applied to any given race or game. A bank of telephones was ranged against the opposite wall, with half a dozen men assigned to field the nonstop calls from bookies and assorted private bettors in the field. A cage of welded steel and chicken wire had been positioned in the center of the room, and Bolan's full attention focused on its occupants, the stacks of currency arrayed on the folding tables before them.

And he had found Scarpato's counting room, damn right.

There must have been a cool half million on the tables, and it was early yet. Toward evening, as the action heated up, there would be twice as much—perhaps three times—all ripe and ready for the picking.

But he didn't have all day to wait around. It had to be here and now, or not at all, and Bolan thought that half a million dollars ought to be enough for now.

Enough to put a dent in Vince Scarpato's war chest, anyway.

Enough to make his point, and let the warlord from New York find out how costly Bolan's brand of private war could be.

He moved in the direction of the cage, his tail in place, and he was halfway there before an agitated banker intercepted him. The guy's eyes behind the horn-rims were suspicious, darting back and forth between the sentry and his unidentified companion.

"Can I help you...sir?"

Uncertain of himself, the banker wasn't taking any chances. He could afford the phony courtesy for now, and ditch it in a hurry if the unexpected visitor turned out to be a grifter or a hungry cop.

"I'd say you better help yourself," the Executioner replied. "You haven't got much time."

Another glance in the direction of the sentry, and Bolan felt the hulking gunner shrug beside him, stepping back a pace to let the new arrival stand alone.

"I don't believe I understand," the banker said.

"You got a call," the warrior told him. "Feds are on the way. Stone sends me down to see if you're all squared away, and here I find your operation running like there's no tomorrow. Now *I* don't understand what's taking you so goddamned long. You got a death wish here, or what?"

The banker gaped at him in silence for a moment, searching for his voice. Then, the guy recovered his composure and dredged a whisper up from somewhere in his bowels.

"I got no call," he told the warrior stiffly, tugging at his vest with trembling hands. "I don't know anything about a raid."

"Well, you can read about it in the evening papers if you don't get moving. Look for pictures of yourself and Cleo here in jail."

The gunner stiffened almost imperceptibly, but he was not about to move on Bolan now.

"If I could just confirm this with my supervisor..."

"Sure. Take all the time you need. I'd say you've got at least five minutes left before they hit."

The banker checked his watch and blanched. "You said that you were sent by Mr. Stone?"

"That's right. I'm s'posed to bring him back the morning's take or let him know the reason why." He flashed a chilling smile. "What was your name, again?"

The banker swallowed hard. "Laurentis. John."

"You named your beneficiary, Laurentis John?"

"I don't…"

"You'd better think about it, guy. You cost the man that much, he's gonna hang you out to dry."

"I never got a call!"

"So, maybe there'll be someone hanging out there with you, huh? They'll keep you company."

The banker broke. "There may be time," he said. "We'll have to hurry. Follow me."

Inside the cage he started barking orders to the startled clerks, and Bolan watched as they began to load the larger bills in matching bags which had materialized from somewhere underneath a cluttered desk.

While they were stuffing both the bags with currency, a nervous clerk was circulating through the room and spreading the alarm, together with instructions for dismantling the office in a rush.

As Bolan watched, the telephones were disconnected, dropped inside a steamer trunk and loaded on a mover's dolly for evacuation from the scene. A garden hose was played across the tote board, wiping out the names and numbers that had been recorded on the giant slate in colored chalk. A crate of betting slips was dumped into a fifty-gallon metal drum and set afire, the smoke dispersed by ceiling fans.

And by the time they had completed loading up the bags, there would be nothing left to prove that this had ever been a Mafia bank at all. It might have passed for storage space, the central cage reserved for stocks of liquor which the bar's proprietor could not afford to lose by theft.

The soldier had to give them credit for their efficiency. It looked as if they might have run the drill a hundred times. A pair of clerks were designated runners to dispose of all the coins and singles that he couldn't carry, bagging them and heading for the exit doors in back before he finished double-checking the valises with their load of cash.

Bolan realized he could not afford to hang around the counting house a moment longer. If they tumbled to his game while he was still inside, if Stone or Vince Scarpato called before he left...

The soldier didn't want to think about the grim alternatives. He hefted the valises with their precious load and struck off for the alley exit with the banker on his heels. A pair of gunners flanked them for security.

"You'll pass on my apologies for the confusion?"

There was worry in the banker's tone, and Bolan knew the guy was sweating.

"No need to mention it," he said. "You met your deadline pretty well, all things considered. I'm impressed."

The banker did a cautious double take and then began to smile. A touch of color was returning to his cheeks, and there was just a hint more animation in his stride as they approached the exit and the alleyway outside.

A gunner had arrived before them, scanning the deserted alley with a submachine gun in his hands, alert for any sign of federal raiders closing in upon them from the rear. He stepped aside to let Bolan pass, and the Executioner hesitated on the threshold, turning to the banker once again.

"You'd better clear your people out as soon as possible," he said. "No point in taking chances with a shakedown bust."

"Of course, sir. Right away."

"Good man."

It took an effort to suppress the smile as Bolan turned away from there and made his way along the narrow alley, toward his rental car. He half expected someone in the bank to shout a warning, and he was braced for flight, aware that there was no place to hide inside the dirty tunnel of the alleyway.

If they should suddenly discover their mistake, he was a sitting target for the sentry with his stutter gun, the others who were still inside and itching for a chance to see what they could do.

The banker's phones were disconnected, but there were others in the bar out front, and runners who could take a message from Scarpato's headshed if he called.

The soldier cautiously increased his pace, resisting the desire to break and run for daylight. But he had to play it out, refrain from tipping off the opposition by his own behavior while he was within their view.

A lifetime later, Bolan reached the sidewalk, turned hard right and left, the sentry's prying eyes behind him in the shadows. He was free to breathe, and free to race the last dozen strides until he reached the rental car, unlocked it, stowed the two valises safely in the trunk. He was behind the wheel and pulling into traffic when he finally knew that he was clear, the neighborhood saloon a dwindling image in his rearview mirror.

And he had sent another message to Scarpato, although it might be some time before the word reached home. He could imagine the Manhattan thug's reaction, and the soldier wished he could have witnessed it in person, sure.

But that would have to wait.

He still had other stops to make before he faced Scarpato once again. More cages left to rattle in St. Louis, different pressure points to lean on, sending home the word that he was still around and still determined to recover Bonnie Newman safe and sound.

He knew it was a gamble, but it was still the only open game in town. Scarpato might decide to call his bluff, or simply crack beneath the pressure, panic, hit the girl and make a run for parts unknown. The Executioner was ready for a range of grim alternatives, with his responses predetermined by the circumstances of the case.

If Vince Scarpato killed the girl, there would be hell to pay and Bolan would be calling in the tab. Scorched earth for all concerned, damn right, and there would be enough of the responsibility remaining for himself when it was done.

But the Executioner still had a war to fight, perhaps to win, and every ounce of concentration would be needed if he hoped to come out on the other side of it alive.

Scarpato and his sidekick, Stone, were waiting for him at the moment, and he could not well afford to disappoint them now. He had a rendezvous with death, and only time would tell if it was theirs...or his.

16

Scarpato watched as storefronts flickered past outside the tinted windows of his armored limousine. Despite the bullet-proofing and the gunners wedged in on either side of him, the would-be capo hunched in his seat, determined to present as small a target as was possible if someone should decide to open up on them. As crazy as it seemed, he knew that it was not beyond the realm of possibility. Not here. Not now.

The meet had not been his idea. He had resisted it, insisting that the others come to his estate, but they were adamant, refusing to be shaken from their downtown roosts and relative security. Because they held the power to destroy him if they should defect en masse, he had agreed to their condition of a meeting place on neutral ground.

And he regretted it already.

He didn't like the way his handful of associates had coerced him into meeting on their turf, their terms. Scarpato would remember it, oh yes, and when he had finally disposed of all his enemies, there would be time enough to deal with those fainthearted "friends."

Another thing he didn't like was leaving Stone at home, in charge. He did not suspect the Ace of anything specific...yet...but Stone had demonstrated that he could not make the grounds secure against invaders, and Vincent hated to think what might be going on while he was soothing ruffled nerves among the downtown dissidents.

If Stone allowed another breach in their security, Scarpato vowed that he would kill the Ace himself, and never mind repercussions from the rest. Without their leader the rest were merely button men with an exaggerated reputation, right. They would be smart enough to fall in line once they had taken time to weigh the odds.

Perhaps.

But what if Stone was actually behind the problems that Scarpato had encountered in St. Louis? What if the Aces as a group were moving toward founding a territory on their own?

Nah. Vince was in control, goddammit. *He* had been dispatched by Ernie Marinello to incorporate St. Louis with the New York family, and now that fate had placed him on his own, he meant to claim it for himself.

But first he had to make his flanks secure, and if that meant exposure to the hostile guns well, he had faced the heat before and doubtless would again.

The limo slowed, the driver changing lanes, and they were sliding in against the curb, outside a high-rise tower of steel and glass that housed Scarpato's largest front, a paper real-estate concern that served him as a holding company for varied interests in St. Louis.

His wheelman left the engine running as the gunner on Scarpato's right went EVA, remaining close beside the open door and scanning both sides of the street, the windows overhead, before he signaled for his capo to proceed.

"It's clear."

Scarpato hit the sidewalk, made a beeline for the glass revolving doors and did not slow his pace until he was inside the air-conditioned lobby, surrounded by his small phalanx of gunners. They reached the elevators and huddled there, waiting until the doors hissed open on an empty car.

The elevator whispered to a halt, its sliding portals opened on an empty corridor. Scarpato's office occupied a corner of the topmost floor and a burly gunner led the way, securing the hall and nodding to Scarpato that the way was clear. Another twenty strides and they were in the office proper, where the would-be capo finally let himself relax.

The others would be waiting for him in the conference room, and he was almost looking forward to their meeting now. They had commanded his attendance here, and he would let the nervous bastards have their money's worth. Before he finished, they were going to regret that they had called on him at all.

They were defectors from Giamba's camp, overcautious merchants of the underworld who had decided they would rather switch than fight. They rallied to Scarpato's standard when the war of nerves became a war of fire and steel. Together, they had fattened up his war chest, made him strong.

And he could not afford to lose them now.

No more than he could let them dictate policy and tell him when to come and go.

They were important to him, sure, but they were still subordinates. And it was time to freshen up some memories in that regard.

There were a dozen of them waiting for him in the conference room, and they were on their feet, all jabbering at once, the moment Scarpato entered. Smiling reassuringly, with confidence he didn't feel, the mafioso raised his hands for silence, stolidly refusing to respond until he reached his seat and all others had settled quietly in their padded chairs. When they were seated, Vince spent another moment staring at them, each in turn, enjoying how they squirmed and could not meet his eyes.

He felt the power coming back, and knew that he was in control. They might not know it yet, but they were finding out, and fast.

"So what's the big excitement all about?"

His question hung between them like a curtain, separating men from frightened boys. The local operators were already glancing at one another, clearly wondering if this had been a bright idea or something **that** could sour on them in a hurry.

A pimp and part-time dealer named Bellomo found his voice before the rest of them.

"You know we're getting hit here, Vince. It's murder on the streets." A little murmur of assent from several others, strong enough to urge Bellomo on. "We wanna know what you an' Stone are gonna do about it."

A chorus of questions from the others ran around the room and Scarpato waited, letting them run out of steam. The silence seemed to stretch forever, but he knew that it was only seconds ticking by.

"I know we've got a problem," he informed them coolly, rocking back and looking casual in his swivel chair. "The fact is, I was working on it when I got your call."

"So what's the answer then?" Bellomo challenged, glaring at him from the far end of the conference table.

"You're lookin' nervous, Sal," Scarpato chided, offering a smile devoid of warmth. "We knew that Artie wasn't gonna just roll over and play dead now, didn't we? You shifted sides because you saw which way the wind was blowing. Each and every one of you was banking on the winning team."

"Seems like the wind has changed directions, Vince. It's blowin' up a shitstorm where we live, and I ain't sure that Artie's at the bottom of it."

Scarpato felt the short hairs rising on his neck. He fought the anger down and managed to restrain himself from banging on the table with his fist.

"Okay," he said, when he could trust himself to speak. "So, if it isn't Artie, then who is it? Anybody got a name to hang on all this rotten news?"

Bellomo leaned across the table, and the sudden motion of his hand made Vince Scarpato flinch involuntarily. He immediately disguised the reaction by raising a hand to scratch one ear. A small, metallic object sparkled, spinning in the light from tinted picture windows, landing with a clink beside Scarpato's other outstretched hand.

He stared at it, uncomprehending, for a moment. Finally he recognized the marksman's medal, knew precisely what Bellomo and the rest were driving at.

"The bastard left that with the foreman at my powder factory this morning. Wasted half a dozen guys and burned the building down with maybe half a million dollars wortha shit inside. You recognize that medal, Vince?"

"I do," Scarpato answered. "And I know that you can pick 'em up for fifty cents apiece at any swap meet in the country. Whatsa matter, Sal, you seein' ghosts?"

A numbers banker named Aguirre swiveled toward Scarpato, peering at him over wire-rimmed glasses.

"It wasn't no damned ghost that wasted Ernie Marinello, Vince. A devil, maybe, but it wasn't no damned ghost."

"So maybe this *finnochio* is still alive, an' maybe he was in New York...how many weeks ago? That doesn't put him in St. Louis now. You're looking for a boogeyman."

"I'm lookin' for a way to stay alive," Aguirre countered, color flaming in his cheeks. "You know Giamba teamed up with this Bolan once before. It's like the two of 'em were friends or somethin', Vince."

"That's ancient history," Scarpato growled. "Unless you've got a damn sight more than just this hunk of tin..."

"I've got three bodies, Vince."

"An' I've got half a dozen more," Bellomo snapped. "How many does it take to get you off your can?"

Scarpato stiffened, felt the hot blood rising to his face. Bellomo saw that he had gone too far and slumped back in his chair, one pudgy hand extended in front of him as if to block a blow.

"Awright, so I was outta line. But listen, Vince...we're gettin' killed out there. You gotta help us out before we lose it all."

Scarpato's voice grated with anger when he answered, speaking to them all but pinning Sal Bellomo with his eyes.

"I told you I was working on it, and I am. Right now, I've got an operation in the works that ought to see us rid of Little Artie by this time tomorrow."

"Yeah?" Aguirre looked incredulous. "So how's that gonna work?"

"I wouldn't wanna bore you with the details," Scarpato replied, "but le's just say the long arm of the law is reaching out for Artie an' it's gonna knock him on his ass."

"The cops? Hey, what the hell—"

"It's in the bag," Scarpato told them, smiling now, but cautiously. "I've got a man with leverage inside. They should be moving on Giamba's joints tonight. I figure the indictment can't be more than days away."

Bellomo didn't sound convinced. "Okay," he snarled, "so le's suppose that Artie goes away. I'll buy that part awright. But what about the rest of it? It wasn't Artie burned my factory down and wasted all those boys."

Scarpato raised a soothing hand. "With Artie gone, it's over, Sal. Supposing that he has this friend you're all so hot about. So what? If Bolan's trying to protect Giamba, then it's over once we get him in the joint."

"And if it's not?"

Scarpato frowned. "And if it's not, we handle it ourselves."

"You ain't been handling it very well so far," Bellomo snapped.

"Goddammit, Sal—"

But Salvatore Bellomo was no longer listening. Together with the others, he was spinning toward the picture windows, where a sudden cracking sound attracted their attention and a fist-sized hole had magically appeared, exactly in the center of the tinted pane.

Bellomo, startled, had begun to stand, one hand outstretched and pointing at the strange phenomenon, when suddenly his florid face began to undergo a ghastly transformation. Nose and teeth and lips and all were caving in, and the force of the implosion threw Bellomo back across the conference table, wallowing in blood and brains and sliding up against Aguirre's chest before the numbers banker had a chance to pull away.

Scarpato knew exactly what was happening, and he was already seeking cover underneath the heavy table when he heard the distant echo of a rifle shot. Above and all around him, men were cursing, screaming as the picture window shivered, shattered, raining down upon the carpet, and the big-game rounds were sizzling in on target, seeking human flesh.

Aguirre took the second round beneath his chin and it decapitated him, the headless scarecrow body sitting upright in its chair for just a moment, jets of crimson pumping from the ragged stump of a neck before it slid beneath the table with a kind of boneless grace. Scarpato had a worm's-eye view of its arrival, and he watched the dead heels drumming futilely for several heartbeats, seeking traction in a race with death that was already lost.

Another round, another...and the local honchos were disintegrating before his very eyes, their essence staining walls and drapes and carpeting and pooling up against the baseboards. Scarpato watched them die, and wondered how he came to be alive himself.

One of his gunners burst into the conference room, an automatic in his fist. Vince was shouting at him to get down when a giant fist impacted on the gunner's chin, obliterating face and all before it bounced him off the nearest wall. He slithered into a crouching posture, leaving traces of himself along the way, and Vincent felt his meager lunch returning on him in a sudden, acid rush.

The spasms gripped him, shook him as a hunting dog might shake a rat, and it was only when they passed that he became aware of sudden, ringing silence in the conference room.

A graveyard silence.

And it was over just as suddenly as it had started, the echo of the gunshots fading on an errant breeze outside. Scarpato knew that it was finished but he took no chances, crawling underneath the table across the conference room, ignoring all the wetness under there and thankful only that the blood he wallowed in was not his own.

Someone had tried to kill him here, downtown, in frigging daylight.

No.

The marksman who had wreaked this havoc all around him could have taken Vince Scarpato out as he had taken Sal Bellomo, with the first shot of his fusillade. Scarpato had been spared deliberately...but why?

Because it was a message.

A warning from his enemies.

They wanted him to know that he was vulnerable to them, anyplace and anytime they chose to strike.

Scarpato reached the entrance to the conference room and wriggled through the doorway on his belly, kicked the tall door shut behind him, closing off the chamber of the corpses from his view. Surviving gunners rushed to help him up, all sympathy and courage now that death had passed them by.

And Vince Scarpato read the message. He read it loud and clear.

That didn't mean that he was listening, however. And it didn't mean that he was giving in.

The would-be capo from New York had come too far to see his dreams go up in smoke when they were so damned close to being a reality. If it was war his enemies desired, then he would give them war. They would be sick of war and killing when he finished with them.

New York's ambassador was far from finished yet. And it was just beginning in St. Louis.

The end would be a long time coming, and it would be written on the streets. In blood.

17

Bolan found a pay phone near the offices of Federal Express and dialed the San Diego cutout number from his memory. It changed at weekly intervals, but he was always kept informed. The landline was a lifeline, connecting Bolan to his sole surviving family, a portion of his past that he had given up for dead, and only lately rediscovered, risen from the ashes with a new vitality that had surprised and gratified the Man from Blood.

Some fourteen hundred miles away, the telephone connection tripped an automatic-relay switch and rang another different phone in Johnny Bolan's Strongbase hideaway. If Johnny was at home, he would be on the line within another moment now.

The "kid" was Johnny Gray to all his friends, of course. The Bolan name had been discarded all those lives ago, when brother Mack was on the run and hunted by the law-enforcement agencies of every state and half a dozen foreign countries.

Sure.

The first time he had been a fugitive.

The younger Bolan was a liability, a weakness for the soldier in his everlasting war. He was a pressure point the enemy could utilize to snare the Executioner...if they could find him.

But when the name had vanished, so—apparently—did brother John.

Adoption was the answer in those days when Bolan's lady love, Val Querente, felt the primal urge to build herself a life complete with home and husband and a son whom they would cherish as their very own. The husband was Jack Gray, a working federal agent, and the news had come to Bolan in the aftermath of his original St. Louis skirmish with the Mafia.

He had, of course, agreed.

As far as Bolan could foresee, the family name was dead. His brother had a chance to lead a separate life, to walk a different path, without the stench of death and burning in his nostrils day and night. The kid deserved his chance to live in peace, and that had always been the essence of Mack Bolan's war: to give the innocent a chance.

But Johnny had grown, and he had made some choices of his own along the way. When duty stirred inside him, he enlisted as a bold United States Marine, and he had served his time amid the hellgrounds of Beirut. He had been tried and tested, bloodied on the battlefield, and when he came back to civilian life, the kid had been determined to secure a front-line posting in his brother's everlasting war against the cannibals.

At present, he was more rear echelon, a powerful support for Bolan's one-man mobile force, but John had seen his share of action, too, most recently in Hollywood. And Bolan knew that he could count on Johnny, damn right, for anything he needed, anytime and anywhere.

They were alike that way.

"Hello?"

The distant voice was casual, cautious and intensely hopeful all at once.

"Hello, yourself."

And he could almost feel the kid relax, the spring-steel nerves unwinding, slowly.

"I understand you've got some stormy weather there."

"It's getting mean, with a potential for ugly," Bolan answered. "Any word?"

"Strictly negative here. Able Team is committed through this time next week. There's no way they can reach you in time."

"And Wonderland?"

"I touched base with your friend. He sends apologies and says his hands are tied."

"I understand."

"I wish I did."

"It's duty, John. The man has his, I have mine."

The "friend" was Hal Brognola, liaison officer between the Oval Office and the Phoenix Project, which had formerly incorporated Bolan's style of one-man war against world terrorism. When the Executioner had cut his federal ties, Brognola had remained behind to work within the system, salvaging the remnants of a good idea that had been torn apart by treason from within. And he had made it work.

The fighting men of Able Team and Phoenix Force were carrying the fire against their enemies, and Bolan stayed in touch with them when it was possible, without endangering their covers or their lives. Officially he was beyond the pale, but they had formed enduring bonds that only death could finally sever.

They were soldiers of the same side, right, and none of them would lay their weapons down until the final battle had been won, or they had fallen at the front.

"There should be something he could do."

His brother's voice almost surprised Bolan, brought him back to here and now.

"Forget it," he advised. "I should be finished by the time his people could respond."

"Is it that close?"

"Could be."

"Well, listen, I could catch the next flight out, and—"

"Negative." The soldier's voice was stern, uncompromising now. "I need you where you are. You've got a parcel on the way, should be there by tomorrow."

"Another contribution to the war chest?"

"Vince Scarpato sends his compliments."

The gentle, so-familiar laughter tugged at Bolan's heart and briefly made him long for home. He pushed the moment back where it belonged, among the dusty, cobwebbed memories, and concentrated on the task at hand.

He was already home, of course. And home was where the hellgrounds were, damn right.

"I may be stopping by there in a while," he offered, knowing as he spoke that he might never have a chance to keep his word, avoiding any promises he might be forced to break.

"Well, I'll be here."

There was reluctance in the young-old voice, tempered now with recognition of a duty unfulfilled.

"Any word from Baltimore?" Bolan inquired.

They had a contact there, a man inside the local Cosa Nostra family, and Bolan knew that Johnny had been tapping him for information on the coast's reaction to Scarpato's recent Missouri moves.

"New York is sitting on its hands. They've got enough to deal with on their own, and Vinnie isn't winning any popularity awards these days. He's got the Marinello odor, and the families are turning up their noses. Same out here, from what I gather off the street."

"You been getting any rumbles on an Ace called Stone?"

"I couldn't place the name," Johnny replied.

"On any Ace at all?" Bolan persisted.

"It's generally assumed that Ernie had them in his pocket...something like a personal gestapo. They're not too popular with La Commissione right now."

"What about Giamba?"

"Everybody's got this attitude of 'wait and see.' If Artie manages to take Scarpato out, there won't be any tears," Johnny informed his brother.

"And if he doesn't?"

"I suspect the families will try to coexist, unless Scarpato still looks hungry when he's done."

"From what I see, it wouldn't do to underestimate his appetite."

"I'll pass it on."

"Can't hurt. Say, listen, John..."

The silence stretched between, hollow, empty, finally broken by that distant voice.

"You there?"

"Forget it. I'll be seeing you."

"I hope so."

"Yeah."

The warrior cradled the receiver gently, spent another moment in the booth, eyes focused on a distant point beyond the fly-specked glass.

How do you tell your sole surviving brother that you *may* be seeing him, providing that you're still alive next time the sun comes up? And do you bother searching for the words when he already knows the dangers that you face from day to day?

How do you live with knowing that your brother—all that's left of flesh and blood and family—has chosen to pursue your hellfire trail to grim, inevitable death?

How do you keep from breaking down and screaming with the pain of it, so sharp that it cuts through your heart like tempered steel?

Bolan threw the folding door back with a force that made it rattle in its frame. He reached the rental car in three determined strides and slid behind the wheel, relaxing slightly as the engine growled to life.

The kid was not a baby anymore, hell no, and he had made a man's decision on his own. He had deliberately weighed the costs, examined all the odds, and in the end, he had responded to a primal call that he could not resist.

It might be something in the blood, Bolan thought. Or even in the genes. But even as he formed the thought, he knew that he was wrong.

It would be something in the heart, and in the soul that motivated Johnny, sure. A passion to eradicate injustice, rooted in the ashes of a family destroyed by savages. The younger Bolan had responded to a call that he could not ignore, and he was giving it his all, without regrets.

Already the friendly ghosts had brushed him with their trailing shrouds in Hollywood and San Diego. But Johnny Bolan would not turn away.

No more than his embattled brother could desert the field of combat in St. Louis, though he recognized the odds against him, knew that he was fighting now on borrowed time.

A young girl's life was riding on the line. A family, already strained, would be torn apart if Bolan failed to bring her back alive.

Another ghost, perhaps already ranked among the others in his mental closet, waiting to reveal itself when Bolan least expected it. He might already be too late. But if he was...

Scarpato had already tasted hell, the merest hint of fire and brimstone to acquaint him with the consequence of failure to return the girl alive. If he was unconvinced, if he was blind enough or mad enough to call the warrior's bluff...

Bolan knew that he could kill Scarpato...could have killed him twice that day, in fact. But he had spared the man so far, had given him a second chance—this one specific opportunity—to partially redeem himself. And if the mafioso failed, then killing Vince Scarpato would not be enough.

It would be necessary to destroy the mobster and his works, eradicate all traces of him from the earth. He would be purged with fire and steel, together with his Aces and his button men, the infantry and laborers who kept him on his fragile throne.

A firestorm was already building in the skies above St. Louis, tinting scattered clouds the crimson orange of sunset as another day burned down westward, darkening the heavens with a velvet pall. Tonight, the river city would survive its trial by fire, or it would be consumed in cleansing flames.

The Man from Blood had already lit the fuse, and now he wondered if he could control the fire, direct it toward his enemies without allowing it to run amok. He knew the fearsome power of the flames and realized that they could turn upon him in an instant, greedily devour him, if he should lose control.

So be it, then.

He would retrieve the girl, restore her to her family...or die in the attempt.

And if he spent his life this night, the Executioner would not be going out alone.

There was a chance that he could still outwit Scarpato, slip through his defenses and secure the hostage first, before he launched an all-out frontal rush against the mobster's battlements. It was a risky proposition, granted, but it was the only game in town.

It would require that he touch base with Art Giamba one more time, call in his markers with the thug and hope that he could trust the information that the ancient mobster gave him.

If Artie had the answers Bolan needed, right.

If he had not already lost the contacts it would take to find a needle in the urban haystack of St. Louis and environs.

If Giamba cared enough about his life to answer Bolan honestly, to violate the grim *omertà* code.

If not...

Bolan did not want to think about the alternatives. Without a lead, he would be flying blind, a human missile wired to detonate on impact with self-destructive force.

Without Giamba, he could only hope to win by pure, dumb luck. Without a handle, he could never hope to find his way inside the maze.

He killed the rental's engine, started back in the direction of the corner phone booth. There was one more call to make before he brought the curtain down, and Bolan was already running out of time.

18

The phone rang twice before a gravel voice responded at the other end.

"Hullo?"

"Put Artie on the line."

Resentment in the voice across the line, and anger smoldering, about to spark. A gunner, for sure. "He'll wanna know who's calling."

"Tell him it's the guy who saved his ass last night. Unless he wants to lose it now, he'll take my call."

A sudden distance, tempered with uncertainty, the anger slipping into second place, outstripped by caution now.

"Hang on."

The line went hollow for a moment, and then Giamba's voice filled Bolan's ear.

"I been expectin' you," the little mobster said. "You've had a busy day."

"It isn't over yet. I need your help."

"Okay."

The hesitation had been marginal, a heartbeat at the most, but it had registered, and Bolan felt the mafioso running through his options silently, prepared to cut and run if the soldier went too far.

"Scarpato's hurting, but he isn't finished yet. He's got a hostage who can hurt you, and I'm trying to get her back."

Giamba was confused. "What hostage? Who the hell... Did you say *her*?"

"Stow the questions, Artie. Let's just say that Vince is going to have the heat behind him all the way unless I get the lady back. Tonight."

"Well, shit now, lemme think. There is one place..."

"I'm listening."

"A kinda safe house, you know? He's used it once or twice before to cool off his hit crews. I always meant to storm the place, but hell..."

"The address," Bolan pressed him.

"Huh? Oh, sure. Hang on."

A muffled conversation now, as Artie huddled with another member of his family, out of earshot. When he came back on the line, there was a tension verging on excitement in the little mobster's voice. He rattled off an address in a residential district, waiting while the Executioner repeated it for confirmation.

"I got a coupla boys run by the place from time to time, you know, jus' keepin' an eye on things. They tell me that Scarpato's got a woman out there now. A looker. Young. That ring a bell?"

"Could be. How solid is their information?"

"Hey, they lie to me, they're history. They say Scarpato's got a broad in there, it's good enough for me. I couldn't say for sure that she's the one you want. You'd haveta check that out yourself, I guess."

The bait was out there, dangling on the hook, and Bolan circled warily around it, searching for a hint of double-cross beneath the angler's nervous tone.

"You feeling lucky, Artie?"

"Huh?"

"You're taking quite a gamble."

"I don't follow you."

"This tip. If it turns out to be a suck..."

"I wouldn't try to shine you on, guy, I swear."

"If I took time to check it out and found out someone had been stringing me along..."

"No way. It's straight, an' you can count on that."

"If Vinnie's boys were waiting for me, say..."

"How could they be?"

"I hold a grudge," the soldier told him needlessly. "You might say it's a speciality of mine."

"I hear you, man."

"I hope so."

"Listen, why'n hell would I be tryin' to set you up? You saved my ass, for cryin' out loud. Little Artie never shits his friends."

"We're not friends, Artie."

There was ice in Bolan's tone, and it was audible, the whisper of an arctic wind.

"Okay, whatever. Anyway, I owe you one. No, make that *two*."

"Remember that," the Executioner advised him. "And remember that Scarpato has you by the short hairs, Artie. Right now, I'm the only one in town who has a chance to break his grip."

"I know that, guy."

"Don't forget it, Artie. If Scarpato's boys get lucky, your ass is on the line."

No answer from the little mafioso now.

"And if you try to set me up, I'll see you later, when I'm done with Vinnie."

Silence on the other end.

"I hope you're listening, Artie."

"Yeah, I hear you."

"Good. I'll be in touch."

He cradled the receiver, turning back in the direction of the rental car. Giamba understood him well enough, all right, but there was still no guarantee he would play it straight. If Artie saw a chance to play Scarpato and the Executioner against each other he would not miss the chance. Mack Bolan knew his adversary well enough to understand that truth and live with it...if he got the chance.

He still had value in Giamba, and the hostage news had shaken Little Artie to the bone, despite its vagueness. Bolan had a lever now, in dealing with the mafioso, and he realized that Artie's own self-interest would prove to be a stronger motive than his gratitude for Bolan's rescue of the night before. A cunning predator like every member of this brotherhood, Giamba would dispense with gratitude immediately if he saw a chance to seize the upper hand. With Vince Scarpato still at large, the aging capo of St. Louis needed Bolan as a buffer. When Vince Scarpato was removed it would be time to deal with Little Artie, right.

But Bolan had more pressing problems on his mind right now. Like Bonnie Newman, and the possibility that he might find her locked away inside Scarpato's safe house in the suburbs.

Given half a chance, he might be able to release her from her captors. If not, he could avenge her, right, and let Scarpato have a sampling of hell before he sent him on to face the main event.

He could do that, in any case, damn right.

And later, he would make the time to deal with Little Artie and his team.

Providing that he lived that long.

Mack Bolan cranked the rental's engine into life and put the car in motion.

Toward the suburbs.

Toward a lady in distress.

Toward Vince Scarpato's safe house, and a rendezvous with death.

GIAMBA LISTENED TO THE HOLLOW DIAL TONE for a moment, finally cradled the receiver, rocking back into the cushions of his armchair, feeling dizzy. His heart was thudding in his chest, and Artie wiped his sweaty palm along the fabric of his trouser leg.

The Executioner had seemed to reach inside his mind and haul out every secret thought Giamba had been nurturing among the shadows there. The guy had known what he was thinking, dammit.

And Artie had been thinking just how easy it might be to put a hit team on Vince Scarpato's safe house, ready to annihilate the soldier when he showed his face. It was a passing thought and nothing more.

Because Giamba still had need of Bolan's martial skills. The guy was like a jug of nitroglycerin, for sure. If you were careless, your ass was history. But if you took your time and knew what you were doing, then you could move a frigging mountain.

Or a would-be capo from New York.

Giamba knew there was a reason for the Executioner's appearance in St. Louis now. The guy had helped him once before and here he was again, prepared to deal with Artie's enemies and asking nothing in return.

It didn't figure, but Giamba never made a point of questioning good fortune. There was bad news enough to go around, and he had learned to seize an opportunity and wring it dry before he let it slip away.

Another time, he might have cursed Bolan's presence in St. Louis, but a kind of providence had sent the guy now, when he was needed most. If Artie could use the Executioner and string the goddamned guy along until Scarpato was a memory, there might be time to reevaluate the situation, sure. But at the moment Bolan was his ace, and Art Giamba was prepared to play his winning hand.

He wished the soldier luck with Vinnie's safe house, even though he did not understand Bolan's mention of some hostage and the heat Scarpato had behind him. If Artie's adversary had devised a way to activate the law, to use it as a weapon in their running war, then it was all the more imperative that he be done away with *now*, before he got the chance to put the wheels in motion.

But Artie wasn't counting on the Executioner to do it all, hell no. The mafioso still had more than one trick up his sleeve, and Vince Scarpato hadn't seen them all, not by a long shot. There were some rude surprises still in store for the New York ambassador, and Artie was looking forward to the moment when he could unveil them personally.

Let Bolan break the ground, and then Giamba would be free to plant the seeds of what he hoped would be a new and stronger empire for himself and Bob Pattricia. The kid would be beside him all the way—he owed Jules that, God rest his soul—and when the sand ran out for Artie in due time, then Bobby would inherit all that they had built together in St. Louis.

Lately, Giamba had begun to think about taking back what had been his before the other families began to feed upon his borders. That Augie Marinello was the worst, and Artie hadn't shed a single tear upon receiving news that Augie's boy was dead in the ground.

To hell with him. To hell with all of them if they believed St. Louis was a happy hunting ground for any macho bastard with a gun and half a dozen soldiers at his back. The time had come to teach them all that Little Artie wasn't quite as little as he seemed.

He still had *legs*, and he was capable of standing up against the worst that they could throw his way. Scarpato had been lucky, taking Jules that way, but now the shoe was on the other frigging foot, and soon the boys out west, back east, wherever, would be speaking of Giamba with a new respect. They would be wondering exactly how they could have been so stupid all these years, taking him for granted like some kind of half-assed whipping boy.

The wind was shifting in St. Louis, and for once it would be blowing Artie's way. The change was overdue, and he was looking forward to the next few hours, with an anticipation that he had not felt in years.

It would be good to kick some ass again, to gain the old respect that was his due. If everybody played his cards right, he might not insist on too much tribute from the families that had wronged him through the years. But then again...

He thought about Mack Bolan, and what the Executioner had told him on the phone. It might go wrong at

Scarpato's safe house, but any problems there would not be Art Giamba's fault. There would be no way that the man in black could blame him if the roof fell in...if he was still around to put the blame on anyone at all.

Giamba had some business of his own to handle, and never mind this crap about a woman hostage and the heat. While Bolan spent his time pursuing skirts and tying down a number of Scarpato's guns, Giamba would be taking full advantage of the situation, using the diversion as a smoke screen while he put his troops in striking range.

Scarpato wouldn't even know what hit him in the end...until Giamba looked him in the eyes and told him just exactly who had pulled his rotten house down. And he would tell Scarpato that, before he pulled the trigger.

It was only fair.

The bastard was a member of the brotherhood, and he deserved the courtesy of formal execution, after all. It was his right.

And it would be Giamba's pleasure.

19

Scarpato's "safe house" was a two-story ranch style on a corner lot, with windows facing both directions on the intersecting streets. The drapes were drawn now, preventing prying eyes from glimpsing what went on inside. A six-foot-high cinder-block wall surrounded a backyard complete with swimming pool and overhanging trees, and an LTD was parked inside the carport.

A simple recon told Bolan all that he could learn about the building from a distance. To verify the presence of his quarry and her captors he would have to get inside, something that could only be accomplished from the back of the property.

If there were soldiers waiting indoors, he would not survive a trek across the broad front lawn, exposed to massive picture windows and an unobstructed field of fire. He would be cut down long before he reached the door, and Bonnie Newman's hopes would perish with him.

So it would have to be the rear, and that posed problems of its own. To the west, dusk was purpling the sky, an angry bruise that spread by slow degrees to leach the power of the sun and paint the heavens in a range of dark hues. Already lights were showing in the other houses up and down the quiet street, alerting Bolan that the neighbors were at home and might be watching for any stranger's suspicious moves.

There was no time for deep reconnaissance, the kind that might attract attention from the neighbors to a strange car trolling on the street. He had to find a drop, and quickly. He could not afford a second pass.

The narrow residential street curved on beyond the safe house, and Bolan wheeled along reluctantly, his target dwindling in the rental's mirror. Then he spied the unattended house another sixty yards downrange.

The porch was littered with the uncollected daily papers of a week or more, and days-old mail protruded from the mailbox set beside the door. The carport was abandoned, had been for quite some time, according to the fallen laves that lay there undisturbed. Bolan kept his fingers crossed and pulled his rental in beside the residence.

He sat there for a moment, heard the engine ticking as it cooled, and scrutinized the houses ranged along the street, across from his position. No one stirred in any of the lighted windows, no one opened any door to challenge him or jot his license number down. The soldier breathed a silent prayer of thanks for urban apathy and set about preparing for his penetration of Scarpato's safe house.

He was counting on the dusk, coupled with audacity and grim determination to succeed to pull it off. Provided that the girl was here at all. Provided that the soldiers were not waiting for him now, already sighting down the barrels of their weapons in anticipation of a shadow movement in the yard. If they had been forewarned...

He pushed the morbid notion out of mind. No one except Giamba knew what Bolan had in mind, and Artie had a world to lose by throwing any lethal obstacles his way.

Still, the knowledge that he might be wasting time, preparing to invade a private home, gnawed at Bolan, but once again, he pushed the apprehension out of conscious reach. Giamba would gain nothing but a world of trouble by deceiving him about the safe house, and the warrior knew the tip was genuine.

He only hoped that Artie's spotters had been right about the girl.

Bolan set about his preparations with a vengeance now. Beneath his tailored jacket, he was all in black, the night-suit fitting like a second skin. He buckled on a military web belt, using fingertips to check the holstered AutoMag, the nylon pouches with his extra magazines. The Beretta was snug inside its armpit rig, the custom silencer in place. The pockets of his skinsuit held stilettos, wire garrotes...the other tools of silent death.

And silence was important to Bolan on this probe. He needed stealth to get inside the house, to find the girl before she could be sacrificed by trigger-happy button men, to get her out again and past the neighbors' prying eyes. The silver cannon on his hip would be a last resort, and Bolan knew that any open firefight here would draw police like flies around a dung heap.

But he would not be able to avoid a confrontation with the guns inside, and Bolan reached down deep into his carryall, extracting his "head weapon" for the grim suburban probe. It was an Ingram MAC-10 submachine gun, capable of ripping out 1,250 rounds per minute in its automatic mode, this one especially modified by Bolan to fire a more conservative—and more controllable—750 rpm. A foot-long silencer was threaded on the weapon's stubby muzzle; it would cut the Ingram's chain-saw racket back to something like the sound of ripping cloth, inaudible outside the target house.

If he got inside.

The soldier left his topcoat, exited the rental car and stood in the carport for a moment, scanning back along the street.

He slipped one arm inside a bandolier of Ingram magazines, the pouches slung diagonally across his chest from right to left, positioned so they left his holstered sidearms free and clear in an emergency.

He moved along the carport's shadowed length until he reached a wooden gate that opened on the silent home's enclosed backyard. He reached across to find the latch, alert for any sound that would betray a watchdog, waiting for a taste of this intruder's flesh.

No sound, no movement, and the latch was not secured with a lock of any kind. The soldier slipped inside, at last beyond the reach of any prying eyes.

The car could not be camouflaged, of course, and it would be enough to tip the neighbors off that something was amiss...if any of them took the time to look. So far he had encountered nothing that would lead him to believe the local residents cared much for anything beyond their own well-tended property. And for once Bolan offered up a prayer for selfishness.

A narrow grassy pathway led from the carport to the main yard. Bolan followed the path, prepared for any unexpected challenge on the way, and was relieved to find that his initial hunch had been correct. The yard abutted on Scarpato's safe house from the rear, and drooping branches from an overhanging tree would offer him the avenue of silent entry he required.

Across the yard in long, determined strides, and Bolan hit a crouch beneath the common wall of cinder blocks, his Ingram at the ready. After several moments he began to breathe again, and risked a straining glance across the wall, inside Scarpato's bailiwick.

A single gunner was on duty in the yard, and he was plainly not expecting any company. Reclining on a chaise longue, jacket open to accommodate the holstered pistol underneath his arm, he seemed about to doze when Bolan spied him from a distance in the creeping dusk.

The warrior could have taken him from there with a silenced Beretta, but there was still a chance that he might call a warning to the others on the inside as he died.

The Executioner realized he needed a diversion, something to attract the sentry's notice short of causing him to sound a general alarm, and after several seconds Bolan found his answer in a row of empty trash cans ranged along the far perimeter. The nighthitter selected half a dozen decorative pebbles that had been used to line the flower bed in which he stood and slipped them in a pocket of his skinsuit, let the Ingram dangle from one shoulder on its sling as he prepared to scale the wall.

He used the overhanging branches of the tree next door to good advantage, scrambling up the six-foot wall with their support and melding with the leafy shadows there, a gliding dark shape more or less invisible at any distance. Once he found his perch, the Executioner withdrew his little cache of stones, calculating distance to the row of targets on the far side of the yard.

His first pitch missed the nearest trash can by a fraction of an inch, rebounding off the cinder blocks and falling silently into the grass. The second was on target, pinging off the pie-pan lid of number two just loud enough to do the job he had in mind.

The sentry came erect, one hand inside his jacket as he scanned the yard with narrowed eyes. When the metallic noise was not repeated he stood up and moved across the patio in the direction of the trash cans, pausing to inspect the access gate that had been firmly padlocked shut. No one had breached the gate, no one was anywhere in sight, but something had disturbed him on the brink of slumber, and the guard could not relax until he knew precisely what it was.

The gunner started on a walking circuit of the fence, occasionally pausing, rising on his toes to peer across and into adjacent yards. Both hands were at his sides now, but he would be able to produce the gun and open fire immediately if the need arose. It would be Bolan's task to guarantee that this one never got the chance.

Slowly the gunner made his way to Bolan's tree and hesitated below, working out the stiffness with a yawning stretch that brought both hands above his head. The straining fists were almost in Bolan's face as he lay prone along the limb above his quarry's head. He might have reached down easily and grasped the gunner's wrists, but any move that left the sentry time to shout would be a clumsy brand of suicide.

The wire garrote was in Bolan's hands before a conscious thought had formed inside his mind.

The sentry dropped his arms, relaxed, and he was fishing in his pockets now, perhaps for cigarettes, whatever. He was looking back along the fence, away from Bolan, his back presented to the Executioner as an inviting target in the dusk. It would require split-second timing and precision, but it was not impossible.

The warrior moved. His legs were wrapped around the horizontal branch, his ankles crossed, and he allowed the force of gravity to drag him down, his body suddenly inverted, slothlike, as he let go with his hands. Those hands were snaking downward with the thin piano wire strung between them like a hunting spider's silken snare. He dropped the noose across the sentry's head and brought it tight beneath his chin, the muscles of his arms and shoulders knotting with the strain now as he hoisted his quarry off the ground.

The wire cut through the sentry's larynx, severing the jugular and the carotid artery before it snagged against the bony structure of his neck. He hung suspended in the dusk, treading empty air, his body racked with tremors. A crimson bib fanned out across his shirtfront and the guy was as dead as hell, damn right, before Bolan released the death snare, letting the corpse collapse to the blood-flecked grass below.

One down, and how many left to go?

No matter.

He was committed, and his target, Bonnie Newman, either lay within those walls, or she did not.

Whichever way it went, the Executioner would have to find out for himself. Inside.

He dropped in a combat crouch beside the tree trunk, merging with its shadow, steady eyes upon the house. If anyone inside had seen their comrade's air dance, they would certainly have sounded the alarm by now. When thirty seconds passed without a warning shout or any hostile guns emerging from the house, Bolan knew that he was in the clear.

So far.

His entry to the house would be another thing entirely, and there was no time to lose. Each second wasted now increased the odds against him, put him closer to the lethal point of no return.

He circled wide along the fence, and gave the open patio a healthy berth. There was no point in barging in on unknown numbers of the enemy, attracting concentrated fire before he had a chance to check the layout of the house. Around the side, a trellis choked with ivy offered access to the second floor. A lighted window, open on the night, beckoned to Bolan as he stood below it, weighing odds and listening to doomsday numbers falling in his mind.

He scrambled up the trellis, trusting it to hold his weight, aware that any neighbor chancing to observe him now, the Ingram slung across his back, would surely telephone police. Another risk, but one that he would have to bear if he was going to see the mission through.

It was a bedroom window, Bolan discovered, when he was close enough to risk a glance above the sill. The furnishings were sparse: a bed, a single armchair, nothing in the way of dressers or a chest of drawers. Directly opposite, two doors were set into the wall a yard apart. One of them, closed, would be the bedroom's entryway; the other, standing open now, revealed a tiny bathroom barely large enough for toilet, sink and shower stall.

The room's two occupants were facing each other near the bed. The man was heavyset, of average height, his shoulder holster worn above a dress shirt with the sleeves rolled up above his hairy forearms. Facing him, a mix of panic and defiance written on her features, was a girl the soldier recognized as Bonnie Newman.

A dinner tray was sitting on the bed, the meal untouched, and from the grim expression on the gunner's face, he didn't relish playing waiter to his unwilling guest. It took a heartbeat for the Executioner to realize that they were speaking, and he strained his ears to catch their words, his face pressed close against the dusty window screen.

"You wanna starve yourself, it's fine with me," Scarpato's man was saying, sweeping one big hand in the direction of the dinner tray. "No skin off my nose, either way."

"I wouldn't touch it," Bonnie Newman said, and there was fear beneath the sharp defiant tone.

The gunner cracked a smile.

"I guess you ain't worked up an appetite today. No exercise or anything like that." The smile became a leer. "Could be you need a little workout, jus' to put you on your feed."

The girl was reading, loud and clear. The sudden terror was an electric spark behind her eyes. "If you touch me..."

The gunner took a step in her direction. "Yeah? Then what? Your daddy gonna prosecute me, bitch? Who says you're ever gonna have a chance to tell him what goes on?"

The lady whimpered softly, backed away. The gunner reached out, a blur of motion as the fingers tangled in the front of Bonnie Newman's blouse, the fabric ripping free to bare one ivory breast.

The Executioner's stiletto whispered across the window screen, its passage softer than the sound of shredding cloth, the muffled sounds of combat from inside. He drew the sagging flap of screen aside and slithered through the open window frame unnoticed, closing in without a sound.

Scarpato's gunner was attempting to subdue his hostage, but the girl was fighting back with grim determination, using fists and knees and elbows in a fierce attempt to save herself. The hardman gave it up and stunned her with a backhand blow that laid her out across the bed, her lip split wide and drooling crimson over blouse and bedding.

Instantly he was upon her, sweaty face inside her open blouse, both hands attacking stubborn Calvin Kleins. The gunner had them open, half way off her slender hips, when Bolan tangled fingers in his greasy hair and cranked his head back at an angle calculated to produce the maximum in pain.

The hardman's eyes rolled up and fastened on the face of death, suspended upside down above his head. He never saw the slim stiletto, never really recognized the source of sudden, numbing pain that traced a path across his naked throat and left it gaping like a second, toothless mouth. The hardman was a lifeless weight in Bolan's grasp, no longer difficult at all to move as Bolan pulled him down onto the floor.

The girl was watching Bolan and her attacker now through frightened and uncomprehending eyes. She drew the tattered blouse together, covering herself, and tried to find her voice.

"What...I...who are—"

"You're going home," he told her simply.

There were tears in Bonnie Newman's eyes as Bolan helped her off the rumpled bed, but they did not prevent her checking out the military hardware that he carried. She was silent for another moment, staring at him fearfully, but when she spoke again the voice was stronger, taking on more life and energy with every word.

"There are another four or five of them downstairs," she warned.

"Okay."

He swung the Ingram up and out, released the safety, double-checked the cocking bolt and satisfied himself the little stutter gun was ready to perform. That done, he stooped beside the flaccid body of the gunner, eased an autoloading pistol from his shoulder rig and handed it, butt first, to Bonnie Newman. "Ever handled one of these before?"

She nodded nervously. "My father's big on self-defense. He takes us to the firing range sometimes for practice."

"Good. Stay well behind me when we hit the stairs, and leave the hammer down unless you need to fire. In that case..."

"Never point a gun at anyone unless you mean to shoot, and always shoot to kill," she answered him. "I know."

Some "kid," damn right. He let her have a smile and led her out of there, the Ingram probing empty corridors ahead of him as they proceeded toward the stairs. From somewhere below, he heard the sound of voices raised in sudden laughter. He tried to count the different voices, stopped at four and started slowly down the stairs.

They would not be expecting death, and that was in his favor now. If they were swift and smooth enough, then he and Bonnie Newman had a chance. If not...well, Bolan did not like to think about the options inside the hostile lines.

He cleared the second-floor landing, moving in a combat crouch, his Ingram sweeping back and forth across the parlor field of fire, with Bonnie Newman bringing up the rear a dozen strides behind. If someone opened fire, the girl would have a chance to break and run, to try the bedroom-window exit route before they finished with him on the stairs.

It was a chance, at any rate. And it was all they had.

Another step. Another...and he saw the gunners now, arrayed around a folding table, concentrating on their beers and on the hand of blackjack they were playing. One of them, a squat gorilla with an ugly scar across his forehead, was about to show his hole card when the warrior called to them across the intervening space.

"I'd fold if I were you."

Four heads were swiveling to face him, hard eyes homing on the source of Bolan's unfamiliar voice. Four hands were reaching out for hardware, grappling with quick-draw holsters, shoulder rigs, the gunners peeling out of there and scattering in a professional reaction that was almost good enough.

Almost.

Bolan held the Ingram's trigger down and swept the weapon's sausage-muzzle in an arc from left to right and back again. He cleared the table with a storm of parabellum manglers, exploding flesh and bone and cans of beer in one fusillade. He watched the startled gunners twisting, sprawling, dying, spattering the walls and carpet with their crimson essence as they fell.

And it was over in two seconds, the ripping-fabric sound of Bolan's stutter gun replaced by a monotonous, infernal dripping from a ventilated beer can lying on the table, and the leading gunner who was sprawled facedown beside it, clutching what could only be the losing hand.

He fed the Ingram another magazine and beckoned to the girl.

"Come on. We're out of time."

She followed him with wooden strides, her eyes fixed firmly on the door, refusing the temptation to observe whatever might be waiting for her in the living room. She had already seen enough death to last a lifetime, and Bonnie Newman had no need of a refresher course.

The rental car was close, across a narrow strip of manicured lawn, beyond a prickly hedge, and they were there within a moment, unopposed.

Bolan took the lady's borrowed autoloader and stowed it underneath the driver's seat. He fired the engine, taking them away from death and back toward home.

For Bonnie Newman, anyway.

He wondered if her home, her world, would ever look the same again, and knew the answer even as the question took on conscious form. This woman-child had been irrevocably changed, of course, but only time would tell precisely what the nature of that change might be. With love, a caring family around her for support, the lady would be fine. She would be home.

As for Bolan, he was moving out of danger into even greater peril, carrying the fire back to an enemy who would be waiting for him now, with open arms. There was no home, no haven for the Executioner. His home was in the hellgrounds, now and always, for the grim duration of his everlasting war.

The Executioner was rolling toward the enemy, an appointment with death. And he would not have had it any other way.

20

The Executioner had called ahead from a suburban pay phone, and the Newman home was ablaze with lights now as he parked the rental in front of the house. Before he had a chance to kill the engine, Bonnie Newman had opened the passenger door and was moving at a sprint across the lawn. A flicker at the drapes, and then her anxious parents met her on the doorstep, folding her in a tight embrace that was all tears and loving words of welcome home.

Bolan waited by the car, preferring darkness and allowing them their private moment of reunion. When both the ladies disappeared inside, Chuck Newman ambled down to join him on the street. The prosecutor's face was flushed, and he was wiping his eyes without a trace of embarrassment.

"I don't know what to say," he told the Executioner. "I owe you...everything."

"Forget it."

"Never." And again, with feeling, "Never."

"Are you solid here?" the soldier asked.

"I think so. Now that Bonnie..." Newman hesitated, reading Bolan's face. "I could request protection."

"Might not be a bad idea. Scarpato's going to be mad as hell about the change of plans. I mean to keep him busy, but it wouldn't hurt to have some backup on the premises in case it falls apart."

Newman frowned. "I didn't hear that, but I wish you luck. Can I do anything to help?"

"Protect your treasures," Bolan told him, smiling, nodding toward the house where draperies were shifting back and forth, the Newman ladies peering out to watch their man in huddled conference with a soldier of the night.

"I will. About Giamba..."

"He's all yours. Scarpato was the mover here, but Artie's guilty as the day is long. If you can bust him, I'd encourage it."

"You haven't got a deal?"

The prosecutor looked confused as Bolan shook his head. "A matter of convenience. He was the lesser of two evils, but he isn't any friend of mine."

"All right."

"You might lay off until tomorrow," the soldier advised. "I wouldn't want your people walking into anything they didn't understand."

"Of course."

Bolan checked his watch beneath a streetlight, saw that it was time to go.

"I'm running late."

"Okay." The prosecutor hesitated, frowning at his shoes. "I wish that there was something I could say..."

"You said it all right there," Bolan told him, nodding toward the stoop where their reunion was enacted moments earlier. "There isn't any more."

"I know."

They shook hands warmly, Newman visibly reluctant to release him for the mortal combat that was coming. And the prosecutor stayed at the curb, watching as the rental pulled away. His figure dwindled in the rearview and was finally lost as Bolan took a left and powered back in the direction of the crosstown expressway.

He was running late for an appointment, the climax of his second visit to St. Louis. He was expected, even if Scarpato didn't know it yet, and Bolan did not want to keep his target waiting any longer than was absolutely necessary.

Pushing memories of Newman and his reunited family away, the soldier concentrated on his coming confrontation with the enemy. They would be waiting for him, organized by Stone and hard as hell inside Scarpato's walled estate. The place would be a fortress, but that did not relieve him of his duty.

Penetrate.

Destroy.

Annihilate.

It was his duty, sure. And where Scarpato was concerned, the man in black admitted to himself that it would be his pleasure, too.

The warrior had an ancient account to settle, and he was looking forward to the last installment being paid on what had once appeared to be a lifelong debt. From the beginning of his war against the Mafia, he had been fighting with the Marinello family. He had destroyed the family's patriarch, its ranking officers, its Talifero hardarm, and an heir apparent to the throne—but still the malignancy was with him, turning every victory to bitter gall.

Tonight, with any luck at all, he would uproot the family tree, destroy it root and branch. Scarpato was the last ambassador of Augie Marinello's rotten empire, and he had to die for that, if for no other reason in the world. And there were countless other reasons, sure. Enough to keep an Executioner in business for a thousand years.

The Marinello albatross had been a weight around his neck for longer than he cared to realize, and now, with its elimination in his reach, the warrior felt a grim elation mingled with the other battlefield emotions he was long accustomed to.

Whichever way it went, he would be through with this part of it, tonight. He would be rid of all the Marinello family and followers, or they would all be rid of him. Either way, the soldier knew it would be a kind of resolution—hell, a new beginning, sure. For Bolan or the Mafia.

The Man from Blood was grimly, savagely determined that it would not be a fresh beginning for his enemies. Their day had come and gone.

The problem was, they didn't know it yet.

But Bolan planned to teach them, and reinforce the lesson with as much destructive power as was needed to get the point across. Providing that he lived beyond this night, this close encounter with the cannibals.

If not...well, he had done enough already. He had restored a decent family, and he had battered Vince Scarpato's troopers to the point where they were weakened, ready for a fall. If Bolan missed his chance tonight, there would be someone else to give a shove tomorrow. Tom Postum, perhaps. Or Chuck Newman. Even Little Artie.

Giamba was a dinosaur about to face the reality of personal extinction, but he wasn't finished with St. Louis yet. In league with Bob Pattricia, the old fox still had several aces up his sleeve, but when this night was through, he might find out that someone had abruptly changed the rules of play. Giamba wasn't dealing anymore, and come tomorrow, it would be his time to raise the limit, or to fold and fade away.

Whatever happened to Giamba and Pattricia, the soldier's targets for tonight were Vince Scarpato and the Ace called Stone.

It could go either way, Mack Bolan knew, and he was ready now. His mind was totally divorced from fear, from apprehension and misgivings, as he drove his rental toward the killing grounds. Another hour, two at most, and it would be decided, written on the city's face in fire and blood.

The Executioner was moving toward a confrontation with his destiny, and he could only hope that Fate, the Universe...whatever...would be watching, caring how it all turned out.

The soldier would do everything he could, within the limits of his strength and armament, his martial skills, but he was burdened by the knowledge that there is no guarantee of justice overcoming evil in the end. The good guys lose with regularity, and he had seen enough of that to know that nothing could be guaranteed beyond the eventuality of death for everyone.

No matter now.

The Executioner was hunting, and his quarry was in sight. He let the singleness of purpose carry him beyond his doubts, beyond misgivings, and he knew that he would give his best, whichever way it went. Mack Bolan only knew one way to play the game.

For keeps, damn right.

21

Bolan hit the turf and dropped into a combat crouch, his every sense alert and probing at the night, in search of enemies. He strained for any sound, the slightest hint of movement that would tell him he had been detected as he scaled the outer wall.

Nothing.

He was alone amid the shadows, merging with them naturally, as if the darkness was a sentient thing that understood he belonged there, prowling like a nocturnal predator.

The Executioner was rigged for doomsday in the dark. His face and hands were blackened with camou cosmetics, leaving only graveyard eyes untouched, alert within the shadows. The nightsuit's pockets were heavy with stilettos and other strangling gear. The silver AutoMag rested against a muscled thigh in military leather, and the silenced Beretta occupied its usual place, beneath his arm. The combat harness ringed his waist and crossed his chest with extra magazines, grenades, a ten-inch K-Bar fighting knife.

His chosen weapon for the all-or-nothing showdown was an M-16/M-203 configuration, capable of dealing death en masse. The assault rifle, so familiar from Nam and a hundred different battles in his home-front war, was capable of spitting out its 5.56 mm manglers at cyclic rate of some 700 rounds per minute in automatic mode. Attached to the underside of its barrel was a 40 mm, breech-loaded grenade launcher, capable of handling explosive rounds.

It was a lethal combination, sure, and Bolan knew that he would need it all if he intended to survive a head-on clash with Vince Scarpato's private army here tonight. He had reduced their numbers but Scarpato had enough men left to pin him down and finish him, damn right, if Bolan gave them half a chance.

Scarpato—or his watchdog, Stone—had sentries patrolling the grounds for signs of an intruder. Two of them had passed within a yard of him as he was about to scale the outer wall, and he had waited, let them pass, when he could just as easily have taken them apart with silent rounds from the 93-R.

But a premature engagement would alert the hostile guns and bring them out in force, preventing him from achieving what he had already come so far and risked so much to do.

Three hundred yards to go before he reached the house, with scattered trees and shrubbery for cover on the way. From where he stood, he could see the house, ablaze with floodlights front and back. The gunners would be concentrated there, he knew, but others would still be roving the grounds.

How many?

No matter.

The Executioner had played against long odds before. It was the sort of game he understood, excelled at, in a way few other men could match. The game of life and death, where you could only go for broke or fold, and folding was the same as suicide.

Bolan was a master of the game, because he realized it wasn't any kind of game at all. It was reality, with living, breathing men and women hanging in the balance every time he took the field. He fought for them, and for the future they would build, given time and half a chance.

His enemies were human, too, of course, but they had forfeited their right to humane treatment by their own abandonment of all humanity. By choice they had become a breed apart: a predatory species that could not be reasoned with on any level higher than the basest gut reaction of the carnivore. They understood rapaciousness and greed. They understood survival of the fittest, right, and Bolan recognized early that he couldn't compete with savages while following the rules of civilized society.

The Executioner was ready to stop these savages. If Bolan had his way, not one of them would leave the grounds alive. And if he failed he would take some cannibals with him, bet your ass. And any who survived him would recall this night with fear and trembling to their dying day.

Like a gliding dark thing, clinging to the night he moved silently in the direction of the house. In the direction of Scarpato, sure, and Stone.

SCARPATO DRAINED HIS WHISKEY GLASS, then pushed it away from him, across the bar. He turned and paced the study floor, fingers entwined behind his back. He might have been a first-time father, walking off his nerves outside the delivery room, but something in his scowl bespoke preoccupation with a darker train of thought—with death instead of newborn life.

The windows of the study had been hastily replaced that afternoon, and now the drapes were drawn, shutting out the night. His soldiers were outside on patrol, but still Scarpato could not shake a certain feeling of uneasiness...almost a premonition of impending doom.

So goddamned much had happened since last night, and none of it had done him any good. One minute he was looking at the finish line, with Art Giamba hanging on the ropes, and then, without a warning, everything was upside down. His world was crumbling around him, and he didn't have the first idea of how to put the brakes on.

Picking up the Newman kid had been an inspiration, certainly that should logically have put Scarpato back on top. Her father had been ready to comply with anything they asked, and by this time tomorrow, Giamba's family should have been a fading memory.

Except that everything went wrong on the snatch. Again. His soldiers had been sitting on the girl, awaiting word from home, and suddenly they all were dead, the bitch was gone.

Scarpato shook his head and cursed under his breath. There had to be an explanation for the sudden turn of fortune. If he only knew...

Of course, there was the Bolan theory, and it made a certain kind of sense. The guy was nuts enough to take on an army and mean enough to make it stick; he had already proved that how many times? And yet...

Scarpato's mind came back to Stone, and once again he felt the burning in his stomach as he thought about the cocky Ace. If he was behind this mess, if he was setting up his capo, then Scarpato had to find out and take action now, before it was too late.

Unless it was too late already.

A rapping at the study door, and Vince Scarpato spun to face it, fairly snarling.

"What is it?"

Stone was in the doorway, smiling at him narrowly, that friggin' smile that made Scarpato want to rearrange his face with something long and sharp.

"Just checking in to let you know everything's cool outside. There anything you need?"

Scarpato snorted.

"I could use Giamba's head, for openers," he snapped, and he was pleased to see Stone lose the smirking little grin. "An' I could use this fuckin' Bolan's head. That is, if he was ever here at all."

Stone paled visibly.

"He'll be here, Vince. Just give it some time. You've got my word."

"I had your goddamn word that we could hold the Newman broad! Half a dozen soldiers thrown away like so much garbage, and the bitch jus' waltzes out like there was nothin' to it.''

He was winding up, and it felt good. The Ace stood silent in the face of Vincent's sudden rage.

"So tell me, Stone, how many men we gonna lose tonight? Or are we gonna lose 'em all? You got a word for *that*?''

"Hey, easy, huh, Vince? You know this Bolan. The guy's a wild card, right? It figures we were gonna take some hits before we pinned him down.''

Scarpato felt the color rising in his cheeks.

"It looks to me like we've been takin' hits all day," he growled. "You wanna count the boys he hit so hard they won't be gettin' up again? So when we gonna pin this bastard down? You got a time for me on that? You got a day?''

"He'll be here, Vince. It's like a pattern with the guy, you know? I made a study of this thing.''

"What kind of grades you pullin' lately?''

Stone ignored the barb and forged ahead.

"He tried to make us spring the girl, okay? We didn't budge. So now he's got the girl, but this guy still has scores to settle. He'll be coming in here, sure as shit. Tonight.''

"You say," Scarpato sneered. "An le's suppose you're right. Then what? You think we've got enough men left to pin Bolan down?''

"I'm sure of it," the Ace replied. "I'd bet my life.''

"You have," Scarpato told him. "Yeah, you've done exactly that. Because if this guy doesn't show, or if he shows and we can't whack him out, I'm gonna have your head. You readin' me?''

"I hear you, Vince.''

The voice was distant now, no longer nervous, but detached somehow. It made Scarpato queasy when the Black Ace talked that way. He wondered if he ought to take Stone now, before he had a chance to pull some other asshole stunt and fry them all.

"You better hear me, Stone," he snapped. "You better hear me loud an' clear, because—"

The sudden stutter of an automatic weapon erupted from the grounds, the hollow booming of a shotgun on its heels. Scarpato dropped to a crouch instinctively, although the sound of small-arms were still some distance off.

"He's here!" Stone rasped.

"Get out there, dammit! Now!"

Scarpato was already scuttling toward the desk, intent upon the autoloading pistol that he kept there, in the center drawer. He had a brief impression of the Ace in motion, and the door was swinging wide as Stone departed in a rush to join his troops.

Scarpato found the pistol, drew it to him, worked the slide to chamber up a round. Outside, the sounds of firing had intensified, and they were growing closer now. The battle was encroaching on his safety zone.

He would join the action in a moment, but first Scarpato felt the need for one more glass of whiskey. A small one, naturally, to cut the chill and chase the goddamned trembling from his hands.

He would bag himself a wild man, or maybe, if it didn't quite work out that way, he would decide to bag himself an Ace.

And if it did work out, well, sure, he might just bag them both. Two assholes for the price of one, and that would be a bargain any way you sliced it.

The whiskey burned his throat and took away the chill that had been tickling its way along his spine. No time to waste—he had to get a move on now, before the warmth and artificial courage started wearing off. Before he had a chance to realize exactly what his plan entailed.

Two assholes for the price of one.

It sounded right.

He double-checked the pistol's safety, killed the study lights and let himself out through the brand-new sliding doors. Outside, the night was heady with the smell of death, and there was gunsmoke on the air. It smelled like victory.

BOLAN LED THE RUNNING TARGET, stroked the automatic rifle's trigger, and the guy went down, the tumblers slicing through him like a heated knife through cheese. The Executioner swiveled toward the secondary target, counting heads and quickly gauging distance, crouching underneath the angry hornets that were swarming all around him now, dispatched from hostile guns.

Three soldiers, sprinting on a hard collision course, unloaded their revolvers at him in the sort of blind, reflexive fire that seldom gets results. He let them come, and then his finger found the trigger of the launcher mounted underneath the barrel of his M-16. He braced the weapon at his hip, let fly and watched a smoky thunderclap engulf the night.

The pointman simply disappeared. His two compatriots were airborne now, in opposite directions, twisting as they fell and landing in the awkward, crumpled attitudes no living body ever demonstrates.

And it was time to move. The soldier knew it in his bones, and he was gliding out of there, a wraith amid the battle smoke, before another squad of Vince Scarpato's gunners had the chance to pin his new position down. Another fifty yards and he would reach the house....

A bullet cracked beside his ear and Bolan swiveled crouching, his automatic rifle sweeping into target acquisition as a silhouette emerged downrange. The Executioner saw a pistolero taking aim, and then another shape materialized beside him, swinging up a stubby riot gun.

The warrior held the trigger down and swept the rifle's muzzle in a flashing arc, the power flowing through his arms and out the muzzle in a lethal stream. Before his eyes, the shadow gunners were disintegrating, bits and pieces of themselves detaching from the larger whole and spinning into smoky darkness as the lifeless husks were blown away.

The soldier fed another HE round into the 40 mm launcher, breaking for the house before the sentries there had time to get a fix on his position from his muzzle flash. Another forty yards and he would make it or he wouldn't, but either way, he meant to give it all he had.

The Executioner was coming in, and he was carrying the fire.

THE TELEPHONE ROUSED POSTUM from the edge of sleep. He snared the receiver on the second ring and fumbled for the bedside lamp as he strained toward recognition of the small, familiar voice that was demanding his attention now.

"I hear you...yeah...and when was this?" Awake now, every trace of sleep stripped from him in an instant. I'm on my way. Roll out a SWAT team, will you, Ed?"

He dropped the telephone receiver in its cradle, moving toward the closet with determined strides. He was on a blood roll now, and all that mattered was the speed with which he could respond.

The goddamned guy was doing it, for heaven's sake. He had engaged Scarpato's troops right in the mafioso's own backyard and he was kicking ass, according to the frightened neighbors who were calling in reports about a war in progress. He would probably be dead before the SWAT team had a chance to get there.

Tom Postum was well acquainted with the hellfire warrior's awesome durability. The guy had walked away from certain death a hundred times, and the opposition hadn't put a finger on him yet.

The Executioner was not invincible, he knew, but, hell, the guy was good at what he did.

The captain sobered, realized that he was smiling now, and wiped it off his face. What Bolan did, what he was good at, right, was killing people in the streets. And never mind that those he killed were little more than chancres on the face of civilized society. The mother-raping scum were human beings—on the books, at any rate—and it was Postum's job to keep them safe until he found a chance to lock them up.

It was a crazy world, for sure.

A decent man was out there in the night, risking everything he had to keep the savages at bay. That made him Postum's enemy, although the captain's oath committed him to something similar...within the narrow guidelines of established law.

And Postum wondered if all the rules and trappings had that much to do with civilized society. It seemed that something had been lost between the cave and courthouse. Something fundamental, like protection of the weak and helpless from the predators who prowled on every side.

Protection was Tom Postum's business, and if he had to save Scarpato's neck tonight by taking out the damndest guy he had ever known, then he would do exactly that.

Nobody ever said he had to like the job. Hell, no.

Nobody ever said he had to do his duty with enthusiasm when he handled scum and was compelled to call it "sir."

But there was something *wrong*, goddammit, and the man from homicide was scowling as he closed the door behind him, holstering his .38 and heading for his car.

Nobody ever said he had to be on time to save the vermin from extermination.

This time Tom Postum hoped he would be late.

22

Bolan hit the study windows with an HE round and followed through before the shock waves had subsided, dodging a rain of plaster from the shattered ceiling. A rapid scan through dust and smoke revealed that he was alone in there. Scarpato had evacuated, and the Executioner would have to seek him out, inside the house or somewhere on the rambling grounds.

But surrounded by the hostile guns, with riot officers undoubtedly en route by now, he did not have the time to search each nook and cranny of Scarpato's palace for the mafioso.

But he did have time to burn it down.

The soldier primed his 40 mm launcher with a thermite round, proceeding toward the study's exit and the corridor beyond. If he could smoke out Scarpato and his sidekick, Stone, then all of this would not have been in vain.

He reached the door and threw it wide, went through low and fast to flatten against the opposite wall. A pistol barked uprange, and bullets burrowed through the wall above his head with angry smacking sounds. The soldier loosed a burst in that direction, instantly rewarded by a scream. Then he moved down the corridor in the direction of Scarpato's sunken living room.

The house was full of frightened voices, shouting everywhere around him, barking orders, questions, curses. Bolan followed them until the hallway ended, opening upon a living room which could have easily contained a small tract house with room to spare. At center stage, a dozen guns were milling aimlessly about, berating one another, hugging weapons to their chests like blue-steel talismans. Above them, shouting in an effort to be heard, the Black Ace, Stone, stood flanked by two more carbon copies of himself.

And Bolan knew that he had found the heart of Vince Scarpato's army, sure. If he could crush that heart, then he would only have to find the brain to make his sweep complete.

"Shut up, goddammit!" Stone was shouting at his troopers. "Will you just shut up?"

The Ace on his left raised a .45 and triggered two quick shots at the ceiling fixtures, finally obtaining full attention from the gunners below. Scowling, Stone leaned across the banister and jabbed a finger at them.

"We don't have time for all this bullshit runaround," he bellowed at them. "We've got inbound hostiles on the property, and one or more of them may be inside the house right now."

"You got that right," Bolan muttered to himself, and he raised the over-under combo, angling the launcher into easy target acquisition as the Black Ace spoke.

"Get back to your positions now, goddammit, and go through it like we planned. I mean, right now!"

But there would be no more right now for the assembled troopers, not in this life, anyway. Bolan rode the launcher's heavy recoil, screwing up his eyes against the sudden glare of the incendiary shell's explosion directly in the middle of the milling crowd.

A white-hot ball of fire rolled up, expelling coals of phosphorous that burned through flesh, furniture and plaster walls with fine impartiality, igniting secondary fires wherever they touched down. He had another fireball up the launcher's spout and angling toward target when the Aces on the staircase spotted him through the haze of smoke and plaster dust.

Stone pointed at him, mouthing something that the soldier could hear above the screams of burning, dying men, and then the Ace was digging for a pistol underneath his arm. His flankers had their weapons out already, braced in double-handed grips and spitting fire toward Bolan's corner of the room. The hostile rounds were close for starters, getting closer all the time.

He hit a flying shoulder roll and came up in a crouch some twenty feet away from his original position, firing from the hip. It took the Aces a moment to react, and it was still too long to save them from a blazing figure eight of tumblers that impaled them, crucified them against the crimson-spattered wall. Bolan had a glimpse of Stone, his rag-doll figure slithering across the banister and down into the leaping flames, before the launcher bucked again and lit a second conflagration on the stairway proper, sealing off the upper floor.

If anyone was up there now, they would be leaving by the windows, right, or frying where they sat. The carpeting and drapes, the furnishings and walls were burning briskly now, the smoke of their destruction filling the room and making it impossible to breathe.

The soldier pulled back to race along the corridor. If Vince Scarpato was behind him, he was dead already, or he would be soon. But if he had escaped somehow, if he was now outside the house...

And Bolan could not put his trust in chance. He had to find Scarpato and see him dead before he quit the scene. Until he saw the body for himself, there was no way that he could leave. If one of Vincent's soldiers found him in the meantime, well, they say you never hear the shot that kills you.

But Bolan kept his ears wide open, just the same.

ART GIAMBA LEANED ACROSS the driver's seat and punched his wheelman in the shoulder, snarling at him as the guy began to brake.

"What the hell you stoppin' for?" the little mafioso snapped.

"The gates are locked," the driver told Giamba almost desperately. "We can't break through."

"The fuck we can't!" Giamba snarled. "You don't know how to drive this thing, then you move your ass an' let me take the wheel!"

The driver swallowed hard, but he obeyed his capo, standing on the gas and steadying the limo as he screeched ahead on a collision course with tall wrought iron. Behind the gates, Giamba caught a fleeting glimpse of Scarpato's gate man, scrambling for cover as the juggernaut bore down upon him, other high-beam headlights blazing in its wake.

Giamba had collected every gun he had and piled them into everything on wheels that he could gather in an hour's time. The raid on Scarpato's was a hasty move, but that was how he knew it would succeed. He had the impact of surprise behind him now, and Vinnie would not be expecting him this way.

It was a masterstroke, and Artie owed it all to Bolan. The guy had run Scarpato ragged all that afternoon, and he was out there drawing off more hostile fire even as they crashed the gates and barreled on through darkness toward the house.

Except that Vince Scarpato's house was all ablaze with floodlights as if he were expecting company. There were gunners running back and forth out front, some of them pausing long enough to fire a burst at the surrounding shadows, dodging, weaving, moving on.

And what was that smoke pouring from the windows of the upper story. Was Vinnie's goddamned house on fire? Was Artie driving smack into the middle of a frigging firefight now?

The little capo felt his stomach turning over, threatening to empty its contents in a rush. The limo was already taking hits, and now the driver brought it to a sliding halt, still thirty yards from Vinnie's house. The other cars were braking, pulling in to form a rough defensive ring, and all of them were taking hits from the defenders racing back and forth across the floodlit drive.

"Get out! Get out, goddammit!"

Artie shoved the gunner on his left with sudden, desperate violence, scrambling behind him through the open limo door. A bullet cracked against the window frame, bare inches from his face, and stinging fragments opened up the mafioso's cheek. He stumbled, scraped his knees against the pavement of the drive, then found his feet again and scrambled back around the limo, seeking cover from the hostile fire.

It was a frigging setup, Giamba thought, and he had been so damned hungry for revenge that he was suckered into it like some greenhorn. They were surrounded now, he knew that much from all the muzzle-flashes winking in the darkness on their flanks, and it would be a miracle if anyone got out of this alive.

Giamba had a pistol in his hand, but he could not select a target from the winking darkness, any more than he could hope to bag a star by firing at the heavens overhead. His men were firing, but Artie's mind was turning toward survival now. Escape. And never mind that some would call his move desertion under fire.

He broke from cover suddenly, the old legs pistoning, propelling him along the drive toward the broken gates. He heard the bullets reaching for him, felt them tugging at this clothes. They grazed him, staggered him, and still he ran, refusing to collapse. Ahead of him headlights were approaching fast, and Artie ran to meet them now, his arms outstretched, unmindful of the weapon in his fist. If he could only reach those friendly lights, if he could hide behind them, make himself invisible, he had a chance.

Giamba ran as if his very life depended on it.

Because it did.

TOM POSTUM, riding in the lead car, recognized Giamba at a range of forty yards. The mobster came directly at their headlights, staggering and reeling like a drunkard, arms outstretched, and Postum's driver was already braking when they saw the little autoloading pistol in the mafioso's hand.

"Look out!"

The captain thrust his head and gun arm through the open window, night wind whipping at his face now as he sighted down the four-inch Python's vented rib. Giamba wasn't shooting at them, but he wasn't stopping, either, and the strike-force chief was squeezing off in rapid fire. He saw the mobster's jacket pop with the impact of his Magnum rounds, the fragile body twisting, going down....

The cruiser jounced across Giamba, shuddering and losing traction for a moment, instantly recovering and roaring on along the drive. Postum banged his head against the window frame and cursed, eliciting a breathless "Sorry" from the driver at his side.

He put Giamba out of mind, ignoring what the other cruisers and the SWAT team's van were doing to him in the lead car's wake. The captain concentrated on their destination, and the hell that had already broken loose some thirty yards from Vince Scarpato's doorstep.

Men were running everywhere and firing weapons in the darkness, seemingly without a target as their muzzle-flashes lit the night. A ring of cars had formed in the driveway, blocking off all access to the house, their headlights stabbing toward the mansion. And he saw that Vinnie's house was burning now, long tongues of flame protruding from the upper windows, licking at the shingles on the roof. The smell of burning, mingled with a very different stench of gunsmoke, hung above the lawn and driveway like a pall.

The cruiser fishtailed to a stop, and Postum wrenched the 12-gauge pump gun from its dashboard mounts, already bailing out of there before the flashing lights and sirens had a chance to register with the combatants of the other side. A few of them were turning their attention to the new arrivals now, some breaking for the trees and other swiveling their guns around to bring the lawmen under fire, but most of them were too damned busy firing at each other or the shadows to be bothered.

Postum braced the riot gun across a fender of the unmarked car and pumped a round into the firing chamber, sighting down the barrel at a line of human silhouettes. Behind him, members of the SWAT team were deploying all along the firing line, their unit leader barking orders for surrender through a bullhorn—and he might as well have been conversing with a wall.

In front of Postum, muzzle-flashes started lancing toward the new arrivals, peppering the squad cars with a burst of automatic fire. He stroked the shotgun's trigger, rode the recoil, watching as a tattered rag-doll figure toppled, sprawling to the pavement in the shadow of a limousine. He worked the slide, picked out another target, fired, and now his men were firing all along the line, their weapons battering the night.

He caught a glimpse of Bob Pattricia, hunched down between two cars and fumbling with his weapon, but before he could react, a burst of automatic fire had ventilated Art Giamba's underboss and dumped him in a lifeless sprawl across the blacktop. Cursing, Postum sought another target now, unmindful of the ringing in his ears, the rage that gripped him like a white-hot fist around his heart.

And Bolan was forgotten for the moment as the captain fought a primal battle of his own. It was survival of the fittest and, if he thought about the Man from Blood at all, Postum would have wished him well. Whatever sparked the shoot-out at Scarpato's, it was Postum's battle now, and he was in it all the way. When it was over, if he was among the living, he would find the time to sort the jumbled pieces and put them in their places.

And Postum hoped with all his heart that Bolan would not be among those pieces when the smoke began to lift. He owed the soldier that, at least, and if he could not help the Executioner, at least Tom Postum would not hinder him.

The goddamned guy was on his own.

OUTSIDE THE AIR WAS CLEANER, but it still retained the smell of smoke and violent death. A dozen guns were hammering at once, and as he stepped outside the study's shattered window frame, Mack Bolan saw that other troops had joined the free-for-all. Giamba's men, most likely, looking for a weak spot in Scarpato's armor while the Executioner distracted their opponent, pinned him down.

So be it.

Bolan had no quarrel with Giamba's troops, but he could not afford to let them block him from his prime objective, either. If they got Scarpato, fine, but he would need the confirmation of his own two eyes before he took it as the gospel truth.

More cars, now, roaring in along the drive, and this time there were sirens, flashing lights, to readily identify the players as they took the field. A panel truck was hastily disgorging black-clad officers—the SWAT team, sure—and they were falling in along a ragged firing line, one of them shouting through a megaphone before the hostile weapons answered him and everyone got down to the priority of fighting for his life.

From his position at the corner of the house, the Executioner was able to survey the squad cars, ranged behind a line of dark sedans and bullet-punctured limousines which seemed to be the focal point of Vince Scarpato's troopers in their brutal counterpush. He fed an HE can into the launcher, raised it to the level of his waist and let it rip.

A Lincoln reared up on its haunches at the center of Giamba's caravan, the shock wave dropping gunners in their tracks for yards around. Another heartbeat, and the gas tank weighed in with a secondary blast that set adjacent cars and men on fire, the glowing human torches scattering like animated embers in the night.

He turned away, ready to concede that Vince Scarpato must be out there somewhere, in the middle of it all, when Bolan sensed a furtive movement on his flank. Instinctively he knew that his opponent was behind him, leveling a weapon at him from a range of maybe fifteen yards.

"You're dead," Scarpato told the warrior as he turned around, the muzzle of his M-16 directed toward the ground.

"That's two of us, I guess," Mack Bolan said.

"So guess again. I'm gonna walk away from this, you bastard. And you're not going anywhere."

"I don't have anywhere to go," the warrior told him levelly. "I'm where I need to be."

And when he moved, Bolan seemed to melt away, his body twisting in a sideways shoulder roll that brought him to his knees some twenty feet from where he had been standing seconds earlier. Scarpato fired too late, his angry bullets slicing through empty air.

The M-16 erupted in Bolan's grasp, and he let it empty in automatic fire, the magazine exhausted in a second and a half. Downrange, Scarpato took it all, twisting and jerking in a grisly little break dance, finally losing it and folding up like so much dirty laundry on the grass.

Bolan stood and moved away from there without a backward glance. His duty was fulfilled for now, and he had crushed the viper's head beneath his heel. This serpent would never rise again, no matter how the severed pieces writhed and twisted while they waited for the end to come.

There would be other serpents, certainly, and Bolan would be ready for them when they showed themselves. But for this time the debt was paid. In full.

The ghosts were waiting for him as he reached the trees, and all of them were friendly now. Mack Bolan let them guide him through the darkness, following their lead, secure that none of them would steer him wrong. Tomorrow there would be other hostile shadows to face, and he would take them as they came.

But not tonight.
Tonight, the Executioner was going home.
And he was not alone.

THE MAGAZINE OF ACTION ADVENTURE

Get the *inside track* on the *guts* of the action adventure scene. Automag is North America's *only* magazine of this type, filled with action-packed news and updates on everything from new books to weapon reviews.

**Try one for FREE,
just by sending a stamped,
self-addressed envelope to:**

Automag Offer
Gold Eagle Reader Service
2504 W. Southern Ave.
Tempe, AZ 85282

**No risk—no obligation.
See what you've been missing!**

AM1/R

NAME (PLEASE PRINT)

ADDRESS   APT. NO.

CITY   STATE/PROV.   ZIP/POSTAL CODE

Offer not valid to current subscribers.